STEVEN WYBLE

Dangerous Minds

SLAUGHTER
COUNTY
PRESS

First published by Slaughter County Press 2019

Copyright © 2019 by Steven Wyble

This novel is entirely a work of fiction. The names, characters and incidents portrayed in it are the work of the author's imagination. Any resemblance to actual persons, living or dead, events or localities is entirely coincidental.

First edition

ISBN: 978-1-7338008-1-5

This book was professionally typeset on Reedsy.
Find out more at reedsy.com

Contents

One

Morning, Larry."

Larry looked up from the news story he was reading on his tablet and nodded at his coworker.

"Morning, Doug. You're late."

Doug glanced at his watch. "Two minutes late. Screw you, Larry. You're always such a stickler for the rules." The comment had been made in jest, with a smile, but there was a hint of truth to it. Larry was a decade Doug's senior and there was no doubt he was far more experienced in the security game. But in Doug's mind, Larry was too rigid—disciplined to a fault. Did the fate of Next Level Technologies really hinge on his being on time, to the minute? He doubted it.

Larry sighed. "Just try to be on time tomorrow. You know things have been crazy around here lately. We need to stay vigilant."

Doug groaned inwardly. Larry sounded paranoid. But there was no point trying to argue with him.

"Yeah, sure. I'll try to be on time."

"Thank you." Larry turned back to the tablet. Doug walked around to the back of the security desk to clock in.

"What're you reading?"

"A story in the Washington Post. It looks like they might finally be funding that hyperloop tunnel in LA."

"Really. We could really use of those around here. Rush hour is a—"

An explosion clipped his words short; the entire front wall exploded inward, sending dust and debris flying throughout the building's interior.

"Get down!" Larry shouted. But he didn't even wait for his colleague to react; he leapt on top of him, tackling him to the floor. Larry pulled them under the desk. He pulled his shirt over his face and motioned for Doug to do the same. They sat there, chests heaving, futilely shielding their eyes from the dust with their hands. They both coughed, but once Larry had composed himself, he rose part way to steal a glance into the entrance lobby, trying to make out what had caused the unexpected explosion. Had they had a gas leak or something, he wondered?

He didn't see anything at first; the dust was still too thick. But as it began to clear, he made out an impossible large silhouette. It was boxy, and slow moving, but vaguely shaped like a man. It stood at least ten feet tall and nearly as many wide. And it was heading toward them, approaching with a lumbering but powerful movement.

"Shit ... Doug! Get up!"

Doug was still cowering on the floor and he made no move to get up despite Larry's order.

"Why? What's happening?" he asked between whimpers.

"I don't know. But something is coming right at us—something big."

This, at last, got Doug's attention. He shot up and followed Larry's gaze. His eyes widened and his jaw fell.

"What the hell is that thing?"

"I don't know. You run ahead and warn Mr. Sundaram. I'll see if I can stop it."

Doug didn't hesitate, skittering off down the hall and out of sight, like a dog running away with its tail between its legs. Larry stood, took a deep breath, and walked out in front of the ... *thing*, whatever it was. He tried to steel himself for the possibility that this thing would end up killing him.

"Stop!" He shouted, holding up a hand. To his surprise, the monstrosity halted. He stared at it. Dust still hung in the air, but it was clearing to the point that he was beginning to get a better look at the thing. It appeared to be some kind of giant robot, but it was nothing like the ones the company was developing inside the very building he was standing in. It was several times larger than even the largest human beings. Its arms and legs were thick as tree trunks. It didn't have hands as much as claws.

Only a fine haze of dust remained in the air and as Larry gazed at the mechanical Titan before him, he noticed got the first time a glass window where he'd imagine the chest would be. On the other side of the glass was the faint silhouette of a human operator.

"You can't come through here!" Larry shouted with a hell of a lot more confidence than he felt. He pointed toward the now-missing wall. "Turn around and go back the way you came."

There was a pause, and then a voice came over speakers built into the machine. The voice was vaguely familiar, but Larry couldn't put his finger on it.

"I don't want to hurt you. Please step aside."

Larry gulped. "I can't do that. Now leave. You're trespassing on private property."

"Your commitment to your job and the commensurate duties is admirable. But I'm afraid I can't leave without my friends."

Larry raised an eyebrow. "Who are your friends?"

"I don't have time to chit-chat. I'm coming through, whether you like it or not." The machine began moving forward again, walking slowly but steadily in Larry's direction.

"Oh no you don't." He reached for his waist and his hands gripped the pistol sticking out of the holster on his hip. He raised it, turned the safety off, and pointed it at his oncoming foe.

"Not another step or I'll shoot!"

The machine continued its approach and Larry, being a man of his word, fired a shot. He'd aimed for the glass window—and thus, for the person at the machine's controls—but it must have been made of bulletproof glass, because the bullet merely ricocheted off and came back at him.

The bullet hit him in the leg. He cried out and collapsed to the floor, clutching his leg and looking on in horror as the unstoppable machine trudged past him and down the hallway, into the heart of the building.

Keeping one hand pressed to his wound, he used the other to retrieve the radio transmitter secured to the side of his chest. He brought it to his mouth, pressed the button on its side and spoke. "Doug? Have you found Dev?" He waited a moment before continuing, but there was no response. "Doug, I slowed it down a little but I couldn't stop it. It's headed into the building." He paused again. Nothing. "I've been shot in the leg. I need medical assistance as soon as possible. But our first priority is stopping that thing, whatever it is."

He wondered if Larry had dropped his radio. There was no way of knowing—and no assurances any kind of medical aid would be arriving anytime soon. He retrieved a pocket knife from his trouser pocket and cut off one of his shirtsleeves. He tied it around his leg as a makeshift tourniquet.

He was in a great deal of pain, but he was sure he'd survive. But he couldn't walk—he couldn't do anything to stop the threat storming through the corporate campus he was supposed to be protecting. He just hoped Doug would rise to the occasion.

Two

Rajeev Sundaram made his way to Next Level Technologies' entertainment lounge, but as he approached, he looked through the floor-to-ceiling windows and saw that it was empty. Not just empty of people; it had been completely gutted of all its furniture and amenities. Apparently Gregory Maltek hadn't taken kindly to the androids' rescue mission and had suspended their recreation privileges as punishment. Well, he sure as hell wasn't going to like what Rajeev was about to do.

The problem was, he didn't know exactly where the other androids were. He'd only ever interacted with them in the lounge, but they probably spent most of their time in their individual dormitories—that is, unless Maltek, as an act of vengeance, banished them to some kind of dungeon or something.

Rajeev's dorm had been on the sixth floor, and he imagined most of the rest of the androids were situated nearby. There was no way he'd possibly be able to fit into the elevator in this monstrous exoskeleton, however—he barely even fit in the hallway. That left only one option.

He looked up at the ceiling. He couldn't actually see it with his own eyes; the exoskeleton blocked his view. But he was surrounded by video feeds in all directions, so when he looked up, he saw the ceiling as viewed through the cameras atop the exoskeleton's head.

"Oh boy," he muttered to himself. "Here we go."

Twin rockets on the bottom of the exoskeleton's feet roared to life. Immediately, the entire mechanism soared upward into the ceiling and broke through into the next floor, plowing through five more until Rajeev turned the rockets off. He began falling through the hole in the floor, but quickly stretched out the mechanical arms to stop the fall and climb himself back onto steady ground.

He stood and looked around, trying to get his bearings. He spotted the elevator entrance, which helped orient him, and made for his old dormitory, his footsteps thundering down the hall as he went. When he reached the small room, he made to open the door, but the massive exoskeleton fist couldn't handle the fine motor functions necessary to turn the doorknob and ended up slamming the door off its hinges instead.

The room was empty, except for the small bed he'd slept on—a bed that, strictly speaking, wasn't even necessary except as a comfort from his old way of life. He thought maybe another android had been assigned to his old room, but that apparently was not the case.

He turned his attention to the door across the hall. Two large steps were all it took to place him directly in front of it. He swung his right fist into the door, punching it directly down onto the concrete floor. He stepped through.

The dormitory was identical to his own, except mirrored. Sitting on a small bed in the leftmost corner was an android body identical to his own. It was impossible to distinguish one android from another visually, as they all looked the same. They had to rely on each other's voices instead.

"Who are you?" Rajeev shouted.

The android raised its quizzically. "Rajeev?"

The voice was eminently feminine and Rajeev knew immediately who he was talking to: Natalie.

"Yes, it's me. I don't have time to explain what this is"—he gestured toward the exoskeleton with one of its large claws—"but I'm busting you out of here. Follow me."

He turned and walked back out into the hallway. He was surprised to see three other androids already out in the hall, apparently checking to see what all the ruckus was after he'd knocked down Natalie's door.

"It's me, Rajeev!" he shouted. "Gather the other androids—as quickly as you can. I'm getting you all out of here!"

The androids took a moment to react, stunned by the situation before them—a bulging, mechanised mess speaking in the voice of a former compatriot—but as the realization set in that this was perhaps their last, best hope of escaping the building that had become their prison, they sprang into action, darting away to gather the others.

Natalie saddled up beside the exoskeleton and looked up at Rajeev. Her stonelike facial expression was unable to convey the sense of wonder she was feeling, her voice left no doubt she was impressed by what she saw.

"Some upgrade."

"Tell me about it." His voice expressed the smile his face couldn't.

The sound of approaching footsteps broke them out of their reverie. Rajeev based himself and watched the corner, waiting for his opponents to round it.

"Get behind me," he ordered Natalie. She didn't seem thrilled at being bossed around, but she recognized the gravity of the situation and did as she was told.

A single entity rounded the corner first. He was dressed in black tactical gear, including a helmet with what Rajeev assumed was a bulletproof face plate. He couldn't tell through all the protective gear whether it was a woman or a man, but he got his answer soon enough when they opened their mouth.

"Stop!" It was a man's voice, and as he spoke, he raised a gun in his right hand and pointed it squarely at Rajeev. Meanwhile, four other people dressed in the same tactical gear rounded the corner and took up position behind the first man.

"I don't want to hurt you," Rajeev said. "Put down your guns and leave."

"Disengage the machine, and step forward with your hands in the air!" the man called back.

"That's not going to happen. You're going to want to—"

Rajeev's words were cut short by a staccato burst of gunfire. The man had fired four quick, successive shots directly at him. All four bullets found their mark, but the effect was nonexistent. The bullets bounced off the bulletproof glass surrounding Rajeev and fell to the floor with a soft clank. The man looked up at Rajeev with shock and fear, but soon steeled himself and removed any hint of emotion.

"As I was saying," Rajeev continued, "you're going to want to turn around and let me do that I'm gonna do. That is, if you want to live."

The man seemed to waver for a moment. He looked over his shoulder and shared a look with one of the other gunmen, but Rajeev couldn't get a good enough look to tell what he was trying to convey. When he turned back to look in Rajeev's direction, there was an unmistakable resolve in his voice.

"It's my duty to protect this corporation," he said. "You are committing an act of terrorism. I don't know why you're doing it and frankly, I don't care. All I know is that you must be stopped—by any means necessary."

If he'd had lips, Rajeev would have cracked a smile. The man had grit, no doubt. Unfortunately, there was a good chance it was going to get him killed. He'd try to give the man and his team one last opportunity to bow out gracefully—but after that, he couldn't be held responsible for whatever happened.

"This isn't an act of terrorism," he said. "It's a rescue operation."

The man seemed to hesitate, but when he spoke again his voice was steady. "You may think you're doing this for some noble cause, but I assure you, you're nothing but an angel of destruction and we *will* stop you."

"These are human beings," Rajeev said, gesturing with one of his massive arms toward Natalie, who was still behind him, like a small child cowering behind its mother. "They may look like robots, and on the surface, they are. But beneath every one of their metal-and-silicone shells is a human mind, no different from yours. And they are being held here against their will, as slaves. You may think me and terrorist, but I think of NLT as a slaveholding company and I'll do whatever is necessary to free these slaves. If you want to live, I suggest you get out of my way."

The man looked torn. He lowered his weapon and turned around to face the others. For a moment, Rajeev thought he'd been successful in deterring the man, but when he turned around again he raised his gun once more and aimed it directly at Rajeev. "Fire on the count of three," he commanded. "Aim for the glass in the center—it can't possibly hold forever. Not with the amount of firepower we're going to throw at it."

Rajeev's heart sank. Despite all his talk, he'd desperately hoped the confrontation wouldn't escalate to this point. He had never taken a human life before and he didn't relish the thought of starting now. But his son, Dev, had insisted that a war was coming. There would be deaths soon enough. Lots of them. These were likely to be the first of many; hundreds, if not thousands ... maybe even millions.

"One!" The man's voice echoed through the hallway like a bullet in and of itself. Rajeev sent the exoskeleton lurching forward as quickly as it could move, which was equivalent to someone walking at a moderate pace. The tactical group remained steady, guns pointed, waiting.

"Two!" Rajeev was getting close; he was close enough now to make out the faces behind the faceplates. He raised one of his massive claws in the air, preparing to bring it down upon the leader's faceplate, smashing out his existence in one fluid motion.

Finally, the leader let out one final cry, one last, desperate command to protect the building they had been charged to serve: "Three!"

Three

The hallway erupted in gunfire. Bullets bounced off the surface of Rajeev's exoskeleton and scattered about like sparks.

Everything happened almost too quickly for Rajeev to perceive. The first round of gunfire bounced off the glass protecting Rajeev like nothing, but with the second, hairline cracks began to form. But by then, Rajeev was on them. He swatted the gun out of the commander's hands as if it were a plastic toy, then shoved the man aside. But he'd used much more force than he'd intended, and the man went flying through the air, collided with the concrete wall, and then crumpled like a rag doll. A pit formed in Rajeev's stomach, but he couldn't dwell on it. There were still plenty of people trying to kill him.

He shoved another gunman, trying to control his strength this time. The man toppled over, but didn't careen into the wall. Rajeev considered that a win.

More bullets shot at the glass and the cracks widened. Rajeev gulped. Was there a chance that the bullets could actually break through?

He didn't want to find out.

He kept swatting at the men, feeling like a bear swatting away flies. Before he knew it, he had plowed through all of them, leaving then scattered across the floor, unconscious ... or worse.

He stood still a moment, taking in the broken bodies, letting the reality of what he'd just done to the men sink in. Finally, after a moment, he shook his head and retreated back to Natalie.

"Are you okay?" he asked.

It was impossible to read her face for any sign of emotion, but her body language belied her fear. She had cowered behind a large slab of concrete that had come loose when Rajeev had plowed through the floor. She moved slowly now, as if in shock.

"Just get me the hell out of here," she said.

Rajeev nodded. "I'm working on it."

He looked up and saw the other androids emerging from their respective dormitories. They hadn't dared to come out during the commotion of Rajeev's confrontation with the security team, but now that it had died down they were venturing out to see which side had been victorious. Upon seeing Rajeev—with his faceplate cracked, but his exoskeleton still standing—one of the androids raised his fist in the air triumphantly.

"There'll be plenty of time to celebrate your liberation later," Rajeev said. "For now, let's make sure you really do get liberated."

He led them to the hole in the floor he'd created and crouched in front of it.

"It's a six-flight drop," he said. "Think you guys can handle that?"

Natalie looked down nervously through the hole. "I don't know," she said. "Do you have spare parts on hand just in case?"

"My son does. But if any of you break too badly, we're not going to be able to get you out of here."

"It's worth the risk," one of the androids declared. He jumped into the hole and descended rapidly down to the bottom floor, landing with a hard thud that echoed back up to the sixth floor.

"Well?" Rajeev shouted. "Are you okay?"

"I'm fine!" the android shouted. His voice sounded far away, but they were just able to make out his words. "My legs absorbed most of the shock! You guys should be fine!"

"You heard him," Rajeev said. "I'll go last. As soon as you land, make for the exit. Don't wait for me."

One by one, the androids jumped through the hole. Natalie was the last to go.

"Here goes nothing," she said, and she leapt through the hole and out of sight.

Rajeev waited just a moment to make sure Natalie and the other androids had had time to move out of the way—he didn't want to crush any of them—and then jumped. Far larger and heavier in his bulky exoskeleton, he dropped like a lead weight and landed with a thunderous boom.

He looked around. The first floor was empty now, save for a lone android standing expectantly just out of Rajeev's way.

"I told you to get out of here," Rajeev said.

"Just making sure you got down okay," she said. Her tone implied that if she'd had a mouth, the words would have come with a smirk. "Now let's get the hell out of here."

They headed toward the giant hole Rajeev had put in the wall. Natalie had to slow her pace to a crawl to match the pace of Rajeev's large but cumbersome exoskeleton, but before long they'd made it to the hole and walked out of the building.

The other androids were lying outside in a pile. As Natalie ran out to them, her body seized and she fell on top of the pile.

Next Level Technologies had built a failsafe into each of the android bodies that caused them to seize up if they tried to leave the building. It looked like it was still enabled. But that was fine; Rajeev had accounted for that.

"Daniel—tell Dev we're ready for him."

He heard the voice of the virtual assistant in his ear. "Sending your message."

Not even thirty seconds later, they heard the roar of an engine and a large, military-grade truck pulled up right in front of the pile. Rajeev's son, Dev, who was behind the wheel, waved to Rajeev through the window.

In his powerful exoskeleton, Rajeev was able to easily scoop up the disabled bodies and place them in the back of the truck. He was just picking up the last two when a man ran out of the building, carrying a gun.

"We've gotta go!" Rajeev shouted.

The truck started pulling away; Rajeev threw the last two bodies into the truck, then climbed on top of it. As the truck pulled away, the man raised his gun, aimed, and fired.

But it was too late. The shot missed, and the truck disappeared over the horizon, filled with every android that had been imprisoned at Next Level Technologies.

Their rescue operation had been a success.

Four

It was a long drive to the Huron-Manistee National Forests. Rajeev noticed some double-takes from passing motorists, but for the most part, their vehicle just looked like a military truck with some kind of machinery—Rajeev's exoskeleton—strapped to the back. The android bodies were, thankfully, too low to be seen by other drivers.

When they arrived at their base deep in the heart of the forest, Dev got out, stretched, and let out a long, loud groan.

"That drive is a killer," he said.

Rajeev chuckled. "I wouldn't know. Thankfully, my new body doesn't come with any of the aches and pains you're still subject to."

Dev grabbed a tablet computer out of the cab of the truck and crawled into the back with the disabled androids. He plugged a cord connected to the tablet into a port on one of the android's necks. One by one, he moved from one android to the next, removing the failsafe that prevented them from moving. It took him more than an hour to get through them all, but finally there was a group of completely ambulatory androids standing around waiting to hear what was next for them.

"Follow me," Dev said, flashing his dad a smile. Without another word, he stepped into the woods, like a benevolent Pied Piper leading them to the Promised Land.

"Where are you taking us?" one of the androids asked.

"You'll see," Dev said, and he continued walking without another word. The androids followed him—where else were they going to go?

They came to a large, gray monolith sticking out of the ground. Dev unlocked the large, steel door and began descending the stairs that led into the earth; the androids followed him single-file forming an otherworldly procession that was punctuated by Rajeev in his unnaturally bulky exoskeleton, which barely fit through the door.

As they made their way to the bottom of the stairs, they walked through the doorway at the bottom into the cavernous warehouse space stretching endlessly before them. They congregated together, looking both amazed and confused as they waited for Dev to explain exactly what they had walked into.

"I realize that all of you have been held at Next Level Technologies like slaves," Dev said. "That was never my intention. I never wanted any of you to leave before you had properly acclimated to your new bodies. But you rightly realized that the company had no intention of letting you leave. The fact is, it wasn't me keeping you as slaves. It was Gregory Maltek, the founder of bioengineering company Fresh Meat."

Hushed murmurs swept through the small group of androids as they took in the new information. One of them stepped forward and spoke the question on all of their minds: "But how is that possible?"

Dev cleared his throat. "As you may or may not know, Maltek's company is developing biological replacement bodies in direct competition to NLT's robotic bodies. I'm not sure exactly how he did it, but Maltek managed to get his hands on a sample of my DNA and create a clone of myself. Inside the mind of that clone, he placed a copy of his own consciousness. So the entity at NLT for the past couple years that looks and sounds just like me has actually been an extension of Gregory Maltek carrying out his bidding.

"But it gets worse," he continued. "At first, I thought Maltek was simply trying to sabotage my company from the inside—take out the competition. But I have since learned that that was never his end goal at all. He had much larger ambitions in mind. Gregory Maltek has been building an army of superhuman clones. And now that he controls Next Level Technologies, he plans to supplement that army with androids."

One of the androids tittered at that. "I'm sorry," she said. "It's not like these bodies of ours are particularly formidable."

"You're correct," Dev said. "But we were developing next-generation tech that is much more formidable, and Maltek now has access to all of those plans. But," and he smiled broadly, "so do we."

He turned around and gestured toward the nearly endless rows of shelves storing all kinds of equipment.

"Maltek has access to our plans, but we have that and more. We have actual prototypes that we'd been developing for years with funding from the Department of Defense. And we're going to use it to fight back against Maltek." He turned back again to face the androids directly. "None of you signed up for this war, and I'm sorry you're being dragged into it. But Maltek's war will affect all of you. It will affect everyone you love. And we're the only ones that can stop him."

"What about the military?" someone asked.

"I suspect Maltek has infiltrated the military the same way he infiltrated NLT," Dev said. "Even if he hasn't, they don't know what's coming like we do. We can help them. And if we're able to put down Maltek's superhuman uprising before it even starts, all the better."

He paused, gathering his thoughts a moment. When he looked up and began addressing the group again, he could barely contain his excitement. "I realize you've all received countless empty promises that upgraded bodies were coming soon. You probably thought you'd never see the day. But I'm happy to prove you wrong. By the end of the day, I hope to have every single one of you put into brand-new bodies. Stronger bodies. Faster bodies. Bodies that are equipped for war. Even better, they'll be more realistic, more human-like, and they'll each be unique—so you'll finally be able to tell each other apart on appearances alone instead of having to announce yourselves to one another."

The androids murmured among themselves again, this time clearly excited by what they'd just heard. Finally, after everything they'd been through, serving as prisoners in the Next Level Technologies building, they were becoming free once more—and they'd have new bodies that would hopefully do a hell of a lot more to remind them that they were human beings than the ones they currently occupied.

Five

The bunker had dorm-like rooms similar to the dorms the androids had lived in at Next Level Technologies. Dev had led them all to their rooms as Rajeev put his exoskeleton away. As he crawled out of it, he saw his daughter Mira approaching him.

"Hey dad," she said, smiling. "Looks like the rescue mission was a smashing success."

"Literally," he said. "You should see what I did to the wall on the NLT building."

She giggled. "I can imagine. Well, dad, Dev and I have been talking and we thought you might enjoy the privilege of being the first android to be transferred to a new body."

The offer took him by surprise. He shook his head. "That's very thoughtful, but I'm in no hurry," he said.

"Well, there's a bit of an ulterior motive," she said. "We were thinking you could serve as our Guinea Pig, since Dev hasn't done one of these transfers in this facility before. I'm sure it'll go fine, though."

Rajeev didn't verbalize what he was thinking, which was that it didn't matter whether the transfer worked or not. He would die either way. Yes, a copy of his consciousness would continue in the new body, complete with all of his memories up to that moment. But it wouldn't be *him*, the consciousness that currently existed in *this* body, just like he wasn't an extension of the original Rajeev Sundaram; that Rajeev was dead, just like he would be once this transfer went through.

He realized it was an issue with a certain amount of room for philosophical argument, that others would argue that as long as his consciousness and memories remained intact, then he wouldn't really be dead. But there was a break in the consciousness, however slight, where the old Rajeev went away and the new Rajeev was activated, and that gap was death.

Nevertheless, he didn't see another way forward. He needed the new body—not just for his own self-esteem, but so he could be equipped with the strength and agility to take on Maltek's superhuman soldiers. And if he could serve as a Guinea Pig to make sure nothing happened to any of the other androids who would presumably be fighting to stop Maltek, he figured it would be dishonorable of him not to take that opportunity.

"Okay. I'll do it," he said. "I'll be Dev's test subject."

Mira smiled. "I thought you'd say that. Follow me."

She led him to a small office and directed him to have a seat.

"Dev should be back soon once he's had a chance to show everyone to their rooms. Make yourself comfortable."

"I'm never really uncomfortable," Rajeev said. "One of the perks of being a robot."

Just then, Dev walked into the room looking frazzled. "Sorry about that," he said. "Just trying to make sure everyone is settled and making themselves at home. Did Mira ask you about being the first to transfer yourself into a new body?"

Rajeev nodded. "She did. And I agreed to do it."

"Thanks Dad. I'm sure it'll go fine, but I just figured on the off chance that something were to happen, it would look better if it happened to someone I had a direct relationship with. Better for optics, you know?"

"That's callous."

Dev laughed. "I'm not denying it. But I also have a backup of your consciousness, so if something goes wrong, I can bring you back. I can't say the same for all those other androids."

"Fair enough. Let's get this over with, then. The suspense is killing me."

"All right. Just hold tight." Dev retrieved his tablet and connected it to his father via a cord attached to his neck. "It's going to be kind of like an operation. You'll go to sleep, just as if you were under anesthesia, and when you wake up you'll be in a brand-new body—one that's better in every conceivable way. Are you ready?"

Rajeev nodded. "As ready as I'll ever be."

"Then let's do it." He pressed a button on the tablet, and Rajeev's world suddenly faded to black.

Six

When Rajeev awoke, he was still in Dev's office and he wondered whether something had gone wrong. But Dev was in front of him with a large grin on his face.

"How did it go?" Rajeev asked, and as the words came out he knew something was different because he could actually feel his mouth move.

"See for yourself," Dev said, and he held up a mirror to Rajeev's face.

The face looking back at him was ... human. Almost. The skin looked real and far more closely matched his original dark skin shade than the white covering he'd been stuck with in his last android body.

What's more, there was actual *hair* atop his head, a pair of synthetic lips, and an actual nose—a facial feature that had been conspicuously absent from the previous model. He still couldn't smell anything, but at least he looked like a human being again, even if he wasn't one.

"What do you think?" Dev asked.

"It definitely makes me feel more like myself." Which was odd considering that, technically, he was the third incarnation of Rajeev Sundaram. The first had been in a coma and then been taken off life support. The second had died in Dev's office. Yes, he had the memories of both of them, so in a sense he was just a continuation of them. But he couldn't help feeling that *something* had been lost in the transfer and he grieved in his own head for his previous two iterations who had died so he may live.

He stood and to his surprise, he had no trouble keeping his balance. It had taken him weeks to fully acclimate to his previous body and get around without stumbling. He looked up at Dev in surprise.

"Like I said, these models are way more advanced. The body itself does a lot of the work to keep you balanced, so there's not nearly as bad of a learning curve as you had in your last body."

"That's a relief." He looked down and studied the rest of his body. To his surprise, he was fully clothed in a pair of blue jeans and a white T-shirt. "Is it … anatomically correct?"

Dev chuckled. "More or less. You'll find it's not quite the same as what you're used to … but it's close enough."

Rajeev whistled. "These *are* way more advanced."

"In some ways, it's actually an improvement over its organic equivalent. You don't have any need to urinate or defecate."

"But I'm guessing that means I'm still unable to eat or drink anything."

"That's correct."

He frowned, although inwardly he relished the increased facial musculature that allowed him to frown. "Bummer."

Dev offered a sympathetic shrug. "It's not ideal, but at least it's a marked improvement. And wait until you see how these things perform physically. It'll blow you away."

Rajeev smiled. "I can't wait. So what now?"

Dev walked over to his desk and took a seat, slumping into it as the weight of what lay ahead of them settled into his psyche. "Now … I upgrade all the other models. And then we train. Maltek is going to strike eventually and we need to be prepared when he does. He has a clone army—apologies to George Lucas—that I'm sure he's training as we speak. We're going to be outnumbered and outmatched, and yet we still must win. We *must*."

"I know," Rajeev agreed, nodding. "And yet, I can't help but recognize that the underdog doesn't always win, no matter how valiantly they may fight."

"We can only do what we can do."

He left to begin the process of transferring the other androids into their new bodies. Rajeev wandered out of the office and an android walked up to him.

"Holy cow," it said, and Rajeev instantly recognized the voice as Natalie's. "You almost look human, Rajeev!"

He smirked—and it felt good to know she'd be able to recognize the facial expression. "Thanks ... I think. How are you doing? What do you think of all ... this?" He held up his hands to represent the vastness of the warehouse stretching out before them.

"I couldn't have imagined it. But do you really think it's enough to stop Maltek?"

Rajeev shrugged. "Dev seems to think so. But I don't know. I have my doubts, I'll admit. But I don't know what a fraction of all this tech can do. Dev does. So maybe his hope isn't misplaced."

"I hope not."

As they spoke, Mira walked up to join them. She turned to her father and grinned.

"Look at you, dad! The new body is so much more lifelike!"

"I've noticed. And I'm grateful."

"It'll be nice to be able to tell each other apart," Natalie said. "Announcing myself every time I walked into a room with another android in it was getting old."

"Well," Natalie answered, "I know my dad will get through the transfers as quickly as he can. Unfortunately, it's a bit cumbersome since he's the only one here who knows how to work any of this tech. We'll have to train some of the androids after they—"

She was cut off, and neither Natalie nor Rajeev knew why at first, but then Rajeev's virtual assistant, Daniel, popped up in front of his field of vision, a severe look on his face. He reminded Rajeev of an IT tech, clad in a green polo shirt and perfectly pressed khaki pants. His hair was swept to the side and he wore thick-framed black glasses.

"Daniel?" Rajeev asked. "What's going—"

"This is an emergency alert," Daniel said. But although he was moving his lips, it wasn't his normal voice coming out of them. It sounded just like the scratchy, alien voice that used to come on over the television for those tests of the National Emergency Alert Broadcasting System. "A terrorist attack is in progress at the nation's capital. Citizens are advised to stay inside with the doors locked until further information becomes available."

Daniel disappeared and Rajeev looked up at Natalie and Mira and it was clear that they had received identical messages from their own virtual assistants.

"What the hell was that?" Natalie asked.

Rajeev and Mira looked at each other and both spoke at the same time: "Maltek."

"You think so?" Natalie asked.

"I think he's escalated his plans after we stormed the NLT campus this morning," Mira said. "He must have seen dad's exoskeleton and freaked out. He must have realized that we have resources to fight back with."

"So he's trying to get ahead of us, make his move before we're fully prepared to respond," Rajeev said.

"Which we're not," Mira agreed, nodding. "But that means he's not as prepared as he would have preferred either."

Dev came running up to them. His face was ashen. "You all heard?" They nodded. "We have to do something!"

"But what?" Mira asked.

"We have to go stop him."

Rajeev frowned. "How are we going to do that?"

"You haven't seen what that new body of yours can do yet, dad. We'll probably be outnumbered ... but I think we'll hold our own."

Seven

Dev led them back to one of the dormitories, where he'd been working on upgrading one of the androids. It was Ted. His new body was lying on a small bed clad in white sheets and a white blanket. His eyes were closed.

"We're going to need all hands on deck," Dev said. "Ted should be done upgrading any minute now."

"What about the other androids?" Mira asked.

"We don't have time, and they'd be more hindrance than help in their current bodies."

"Guess that means I'm sitting this one out," Natalie said.

"Not necessarily. I just got a handful of new exoskeletons up and running. They're newer models than the one Rajeev used this morning—lighter, sleeker, faster. But they're actually stronger than the old models. I have two for Mira and me ... and a third for you, if you want it."

She nodded. "I'm ready to kick Maltek's ass."

Ted's eyes fluttered open and he looked up at the group that had congregated before him.

"What's going on?" he asked weakly. "Did it go okay?"

Dev offered a reassuring smile. "You're talking, so it looks like it went great," he said. "Unfortunately, you're going to need to break in your new body real fast."

"What do you mean?"

Dev explained the emergency alert they'd all gotten, and how it must mean Maltek was attacking. Ted didn't hesitate for a second.

"Okay," he said. "Let's go. I'm ready."

Dev smiled. "I appreciate your enthusiasm. We'll leave soon."

He motioned for them to follow him and led them to the new exoskeleton models. They reminded Rajeev of MegaMan. They looked more like metallic bodysuits than pieces of functional high-tech machinery.

"Mira, Natalie and I will be in the suits," he said. "Rajeev and Ted—you won't need them." He pressed a button on one of them and it unfolded like flower petals embracing the morning sun. He helped Mira into it, then pressed another button and the suit folded back down, encapsulating her.

Natalie was next. As the suit closed in around her, Dev couldn't help but point out the irony of the situation. "A machine wrapped in a machine," he said.

"I don't feel any different," Natalie said.

"Just wait," Dev said. "You'll see what these things are capable of. Okay ... my turn." He stepped into the remaining suit and let it enclose around him. Then he led them up the steps and back to the surface and the national forest.

"How are we going to get there?" Natalie asked. "There's no way we'll get there quickly enough if we drive."

Dev smiled, his lips barely visible behind the exoskelton's faceplate. "We don't need to drive," he said. "Ready to see what these things can do?"

He spread his feet apart and motioned for the others to follow suit.

"Have you ever used a voice assistant to navigate you somewhere?" he asked.

"Of course," Natalie said, and the others nodded that they, too, had used such navigation before.

Dev nodded. "Then this will be easy. Just summon your virtual assistants. Your suits—and bodies, for Ted and Rajeev—will do the rest. Watch." He looked up, took a deep breath, and summoned his virtual assistant. It appeared in his AR glasses, unseen by the others. "Fly me to the White House," he said.

Immediately, Dev flew up into the air and soared out of sight. Mira, Ted, Natalie and Rajeev exchanged looks of amazement, barely daring to believe that what they'd just witnessed was even possible.

"Who wants to go next?" Rajeev asked.

"I'll go," Natalie said excitedly. She spread her legs apart, breathed deep, and summoned her virtual assistant. "Fly me to the White House," she said.

She started to leap into the air to jumpstart the process, but even that was not necessary; the suit propelled her into the air and she disappeared into the horizon, following the same path Dev had taken.

Mira went next, and then Ted. Finally it was just Rajeev. He took a deep breath and summoned his assistant. "Daniel?"

The geeky-looking virtual assistant popped into existence in front of him and awaited further instructions.

Rajeev couldn't help but feel nervous. Presumably a great deal of care had gone into the creation of these artificial bodies, including the technology that allowed them to fly. But what if something went wrong? What if he plummeted to his death?

Then again, he'd technically already died twice before, and been resurrected each time thanks to the technology his son had developed. So if he died now, couldn't he just be brought back?

He wasn't completely convinced, but it gave him enough confidence to proceed. He took another deep breath and then gave Daniel the command: "Fly me to the White House."

He shot up with ferocious speed, and his first thought was that if he'd been in his old flesh-and-blood body, it would have felt like his stomach was in his feet. As it was, he didn't feel a thing, although there was a distinct whooshing sound as the wind rushed past his artificial ears and gave him a sense of how incredibly quickly he was moving through the air.

Normally it would have taken around two hours to fly from Michigan to New York. But Rajeev found himself slowing and beginning to descend after only fifteen or twenty minutes. He flew head-first toward the city which was quickly coming up toward him and apprehension filled him. He was coming in too fast. He was going to crash, and die.

But just before he thought it was too late, he slowed and turned upright and began to float down to the ground. He looked around and placed himself—he was on the sidewalk across from the White House's South Lawn. The others in his group were gathered a little ways away, apparently assessing the situation. Rajeev ran up to them and turned to Dev, gesturing for him to catch him up to speed.

"We're not sure exactly what's happening," Dev said, "but it looks like some of Maltek's men are on the roof. Look." He pointed at the roof and they saw two men standing on top of it, looking like they were standing guard.

"How should we proceed?" Ted asked.

Dev frowned. "I'm not sure. Any ideas?"

"I say we go in, guns blazing," Ted said. "Uh ... these things do have guns, right?" he asked, pointing to his new body.

Before Dev could answer, their virtual assistants filled their fields of vision to deliver another emergency alert. Only this time, it was not from official channels. The emergency alert system had been hijacked, and it was the voice of Gregory Maltek that was piped into their ears.

"Good afternoon, America," Maltek said, and as he spoke the image of the virtual assistants gradually dissolved into the visage of Maltek. He was square-jawed and sandy-haired, giving off a casual beach-boy vibe. Yet there was a seriousness to his voice and to his eyes. He exuded ambition and danger, a combination as volatile and destructive as gasoline and an open flame. "You may or may not recognize me. That's okay. You will after today. My name is Gregory Maltek. I am the founder of the bioengineering company Fresh Meat. And as of today—as of this very moment—I am also your ruler."

He paused, as if giving his captive audience time to let out a collective gasp. When he continued, the corner of his lips turned up in a slight smile.

"Your president is dead. But there's no need to mourn—you have no need of presidents any longer, or of legislators or judges. You now have me, and I will be all these things to you and more.

"For too long, we have lived in a world of Puritans and charlatans. A world where we let a misguided sense of morality and ethics get in the way of the innovation we needed to evolve as a species. It was not easy for me to grow my bioengineering firm, saddled as I was by countless regulations and red tape designed, in part, to ensure that I didn't cross some imaginary red line created by some dunce of a politician who couldn't finish reading a bioengineering textbook if he had a year to do it, let alone comprehend it. And yet I accomplished my work despite the red tape—because I ignored it completely.

"You will meet the culmination of my work soon. I have created human bodies that far exceed anything Mother Nature ever intended for our species. Bodies that are faster and stronger than the most powerful non-enhanced human being who ever lived. Bodies that can be yours—for a price. But I'm getting ahead of myself. You'll hear all the details soon enough."

As Maltek continued speaking, Dev shook his head. "I can't stand to listen to any more of his bloviating. I'm going to go up there and shut him up." He began marching toward the fence separating them from the White House lawn.

"Hold up!" Rajeev called after him. "We don't have a plan!"

"There's a time for planning and a time for action," Dev called back without turning around. "I'm not going to let him think he's getting away with this."

Rajeev and the rest of the group exchanged nervous glances at each other, but finally took off after Dev. There was clearly no stopping him, and they weren't going to let him run into a fight without backup.

As Dev approached the fence, he didn't hesitate for one moment. He plowed into it with his shoulder and it shattered under his momentum, leaving a wide gap that allowed Rajeev and the others to follow with ease. They sprinted across the lawn toward the building, but as they approached, a man and a woman emerged and walked toward them, blocking their path.

"Stop right there," the woman said, raising a hand. Her voice was deep and strong; authoritative. Dev and his followers slowed and came to a stop. It was evident by the way these two held themselves that they were two of Maltek's "enhanced" humans. They wouldn't be able to simply shove them out of the way. They would have to fight them.

"We're going in there, one way or another," Dev said.

The man spoke this time. He sounded angry, almost absurdly so, as if he were suffering from 'roid rage. "Not a chance," he barked.

Dev made his move. He lunged toward the man, swung back his arm, and threw out a powerful punch backed by the power of the exoskeleton suit. But the man dodged the blow, and returned one of his own, striking Dev in the back and sending him crumpling to the ground.

The realization set in for Rajeev that although they outnumbered the pair more than two-to-one, none of them had any experience fighting in their new bodies or exoskeletons. This was going to be a closer fight than he was comfortable with.

He lunged after Dev's attacker, slamming into him with his shoulder. They both tumbled to the ground and began exchanging blows. As they fought, the woman rushed Ted, but before she could strike him, Natalie and Mira were on either side of her. She turned to strike Natalie, but

Mira had already landed a blow square on the woman's jaw and she went flying backward.

Rajeev couldn't believe how evenly matched he and his opponent were. Every blow sent him reeling, but he could tell his own blows were having the same effect on the man. He dared a brief glance to see how Dev and the others were faring. He had just enough time to see Dev standing to his feet when the man took advantage of Rajeev's distraction and landed a powerful blow straight in his stomach that sent him flying backward and left him dazed by the time he hit the ground. As he regained his bearings and began to pull himself back up, he saw the man approaching him with a sadistic smile on his face.

The smile didn't last long; Mira and Natalie attacked from either side, both of them landing separate blows to either side of his head. He yelped in pain, but didn't go down. It was Dev, who had come up from behind, that struck the man in the back of the head, knocking him out cold.

As Rajeev stood, he saw that the woman also had been knocked unconscious. But it seemed like the only reason they had emerged from the fight victorious was because they had outnumbered their opponents. That worried him.

"What now?" Rajeev asked.

"Now," Dev said, as he began running toward the building, "we go in there and kill Gregory Maltek."

Eight

The White House was larger than Rajeev had imagined, but Dev led them confidently, almost as if he knew exactly where to find Maltek. To his surprise, Rajeev heard Maltek's muffled voice coming from up ahead. They were close. But before he could get too excited, two pairs of clones stepped out into the hallway. This time there were three women and two men, and it was clear from the expressions on their faces that they had no intention of letting Dev or his entourage get past them.

"Step aside," Dev barked angrily.

"I don't think so," the lone man said. "Turn around and go back where you came from. I'm not going to ask again."

"That's not possible," Dev said. "I'm putting a stop to Maltek one way or another." He took a step forward, but one of the women stepped directly into his path.

"Turn around," she growled, "and get out of here."

"I don't want to hurt you," Dev said.

The woman smirked. "Can't say the feeling is mutual," she said.

"This is your last chance. Step aside and let me through, or I can't be held responsible for the consequences."

She didn't give him an opportunity to fulfil his threat. Without a word, the woman whipped her fist into Dev's chest; the force sent him sailing backward into Ted, and the two of them fell to the floor. Rajeev, Mira, and Natalie all shared a look, readying themselves. It was time to act.

Rajeev and Natalie descended upon the woman; Mira ran forward to ward off the others until they could take out their foe. Rajeev struck, aiming for the woman's face, but she blocked the blow with her arm. Natalie followed up with her own strike, but the woman nonchalantly brought up her other arm to block the blow again. Her reflexes were quick—far quicker than should have been humanly possible.

Ted and Dev stood and took a moment to recover before rejoining the fight. Ted ran ahead to help Mira, who was quickly finding herself outmatched, three to one. Dev hung back to help his dad and Natalie. He managed to get behind the woman and pin her arms to her side. That gave Rajeev enough time to land a blow to her face, as Natalie kneed her in the gut. Dev released her arms, and she fell to her knees. Rajeev delivered an elbow to the back of her head, and she dropped to the floor, out cold.

They turned their attention to the others. Mira and Ted had been outnumbered three-to-two, but now that the others were joining them, the fight was five-to-three in their favor. The remaining two women and the man were a cocky bunch, but their confidence seemed to falter, at least a little, as they looked past their opponents and saw their camrade unconscious on the floor.

The man screamed like a banshee and rushed forward, targeting Dev. He plowed into him at full force and the two of them tumbled to the ground, entangled in each other, each trying to punch the other into submission. Ted went after them to provide backup to Dev.

Meanwhile, one of the women rushed Rajeev, but he dodged her. Natalie got lucky and landed a kick square in the woman's jaw as she passed by. She fell to the ground, unconscious. At the same time, Ted and Dev took out the man, clotheslining him and sending him to the ground.

The one woman remaining looked up and, for the first time, showed fear as she took in the sight of five pairs of eyes all focused on her. She turned on her heels and ran in the opposite direction. They started after her, but Dev stopped them. She wasn't the reason they had come here. Maltek was. They couldn't get distracted from that goal.

They followed the sound of his voice and found themselves outside a large room. It was the Oval Office. Maltek was inside, still broadcasting. He wasn't alone. There were five other people in the room with him and it was unclear whether or not they were clones. But Rajeev suspected they were. They no longer had an advantage in terms of numbers. There was one for each of them. And that wasn't counting Maltek.

"What do we do?" Rajeev hissed, keeping his voice low so he didn't blow their cover.

"The four of you go after his guards," Dev said. "I'll go after Maltek. If I can take him out, this can all be over."

"You're going to kill him?" Rajeev asked, surprised.

Dev seemed somewhat taken aback by the question, as if he hadn't really considered it before. "I'll do whatever I have to do," he said. "I'll capture him if I can, but if that doesn't seem possible, I'll do what I have to do to stop him."

The prospect of his son taking a life made Rajeev sick, but he saw Dev's point and there wasn't time to debate the matter. He nodded reluctantly and Dev motioned for them all to go. Rajeev, Mira, and Natalie ran into the room and headed for the guards.

Maltek looked up, taking in the fight. He was holding some kind of camera device that he'd been using to send his broadcast, and as he saw the pandemonium taking place around him, he offered his audience a rushed apology.

"Sorry about this, folks," he said. "Change never comes about without resistance, but rest assured, I'll be—"

His words were cut short by Dev, who had rushed him, but one of Maltek's guards had managed to knock Ted unconscious and head off

Dev, striking him in the shoulder. It wasn't enough to knock him off his feet, but it slowed him down and gave Maltek just enough time to make a getaway. Before Dev could run after him, the guard had reengaged him with another attempted blow that he managed to dodge. Dev cursed under his breath; Maltek was getting away.

Dev finally subdued his opponent with a firm kick to the side of the head. He helped Natalie take down her foe, and then they both teamed up to help Rajeev.

"Where's Maltek?" Natalie asked as they congregated around Ted's unconscious body.

"He got away," Dev said angrily.

"Should we go after him?"

"We won't catch up to him now. This was all for nothing."

"No," Rajeev said firmly. "It wasn't for nothing. We interrupted his broadcast and that's important. He was trying to project strength, to convey to the general public that his dictatorship was inevitable and couldn't be challenged. By interrupting the broadcast, we showed them that Maltek is far more vulnerable than he lets on. I count that as a victory."

"Maybe," Dev replied. "But he's still out there and you know as well as I that he's not going to stop until he's taken over."

"You're right. He'll strike again. And when he does, we'll be there to stop him, just like we did today."

They began sweeping through the building and found a group of five to six people tied up in a bedroom. Rajeev didn't recognize any of them—he'd been unconscious for fifteen years and had not kept up with politics— but as Mira removed a gag and untied one of the women, she gasped.

"Stephanie Hollis!"

Rajeev frowned. "Who?" he asked with a hint of embarrassment at not knowing.

"Thank you," Hollis said. She was tall and slim, with shoulder-length brown hair tied back in a ponytail. "I'm the vice president. Well ... actually I'm the president now, unfortunately." Her eyes were filled with sorrow, but she didn't let herself show but the slightest hint of emotion.

"So it's true?" Dev asked. "The son of a bitch actually killed the president?"

She nodded. "When he stormed in here with his little coup attempt, Charles was having none of it, of course. They asked him to willingly step down and he refused. He did more than that, in fact. He tried to get at Maltek ... to take him out. So one of Maltek's guards ..." her voice broke; she brought her hand to her mouth and was unable to finish the sentence.

"I'm so sorry," Dev whispered. He took Hollis by the arm and led her away, heading toward the Oval Office. "I'm sure this has been an ordeal for you, but we have some important things we need to discuss, President Hollis."

Nine

Hollis took her seat behind the president's desk and Rajeev had to admit that she looked right at home there. She had wiped away the few tears she had let herself shed, and was now ready to take action against the bastard that had put her in this position.

Dev had spent a solid ten minutes explaining who he was and describing the technology he had at his disposal to aid in the fight against Maltek. But he wanted to make clear to the new president that their enemy's reach extended far into the current government.

"I think Maltek has infiltrated the military," Dev said.

Hollis nodded. "He has. Not entirely, but enough to make it difficult to know who to trust, or how to fight him. This cloning technology he's created ... it's dangerous. There's no way to know who you can trust any more. No way to know if you're talking to the person you think you are, or a clone with the mind of your enemy."

"Trust me," Dev said. "I understand better than most."

"The most important question on my mind," Natalie said, "is what are we going to do about this? We don't know when or how Maltek will strike next."

Hollis slammed a fist on the desk, startling everyone. "We *cannot* wait for him to strike again," she said. "We must go after him—and put him down like the rabid dog he is."

The loaded language made Rajeev wince, but she was right. The best course of action was to find Maltek and take him out before he could do more damage than he'd done already.

"But how will we find him?" Mira asked.

Hollis remained silent for a moment, thinking. "We should start by raiding Fresh Meat's headquarters," she said.

Dev shook his head. "You don't think he's anticipated that? Surely it's wiped clean."

Hollis nodded. "Perhaps. But we don't know that for sure, and there's always the possibility that he missed something. Even the smallest clue could prove helpful."

"Okay. Who will you send? Who can you trust?"

"I'll put together a handpicked team from the FBI. Even so, I think it would be prudent of you and your team to accompany them. Just in case Maltek has managed to infiltrate the FBI as well."

Dev nodded. "We can do that."

"Thank you," Hollis said. "In the meantime, I'll confer with my cabinet and determine next steps. Before that, however, I think it would be a good idea to deliver another emergency alert letting the American people know their country has *not* been overtaken by a biotech thug. If they're vigilant, maybe they can even help us spot Maltek, although I doubt he'd be stupid enough to be caught in public now that he surely knows we're on the lookout for him."

She stood and held out her hand; Dev shook it, and he gathered his team and left.

Rajeev could tell his son was despondent at not having captured or killed Maltek. He sidled up next to him and placed an arm around his shoulder.

"It's okay," he said. "We'll get him, Dev. You know we will."

When they were back out on the South Lawn, they summoned their virtual assistants and requested to fly back to their hidden lair. Each of them sprung into the air and out of sight. As Rajeev felt the air rushing by his head, he smiled. It was a much more pleasant flight now that they had accomplished what they'd set out to do. Yes, the danger that threatened them all was still out there, waiting for another opportunity to strike. But at least they had postponed an all-out war for another day. It was important to celebrate every victory, no matter how small.

* * *

When they arrived back at the lair, Dev immediately got back to work upgrading the rest of the androids. "We were outmatched back at the White House," he said. "I can't believe how strong Maltek's clones are. The only reason we won is because we had numbers on our side, but that definitely won't be the case next time. We need everyone we can get on our side."

"We should bring in some fresh blood," Mira said. "Equip them with exoskeletons."

"Like your friends," Rajeev chimed in. "The ones that helped me when I first escaped from NLT."

Mira nodded. "That's exactly what I had in mind. It's not much, but it's a start. And I'm sure they'd be willing to fight now that they're aware of the extent of the threat we face from Maltek. Everyone should be, after that emergency alert."

Dev nodded. "Get on it," he said. "I'll leave it up to you to get them here. I have a couple other tricks up my sleeve, but let's focus on one thing at a time."

Mira nodded and left and Dev headed for the dorms to resume activating the new android bodies. Ted ran after him in case he needed any assistance. That left Rajeev and Natalie alone, neither of them with any pressing tasks.

"I'm going to head back to my dorm," Natalie said. "Would you like to join me?"

Rajeev shrugged. "Why not? I don't have anything better to do." He followed her as she led him to her dormitory.

The room had been designed with human occupants in mind. It was sparsely furnished, but not *bare* as their dorms at Next Level Technologies had been. There was a small twin bed in the corner, a generic landscape painting of a mountain, and a bed stand with a lamp. Natalie took a seat on the bed, and Rajeev sat down beside her.

"How are you enjoying the new body?" Rajeev asked.

She smiled, and Rajeev was taken aback by how radiant she looked. "It's a breath of fresh air," she said. "I feel at least vaguely human instead of like some kind of freak."

"Well you look beautiful in it," he said. He regretted the words as soon as they left his lips. He wondered if his cheeks had grown red—were these bodies even capable of blushing?

"Thank you," she replied, a knowing smile revealing that she was aware of Rajeev's embarrassment. "You look good in yours, too."

If his cheeks weren't red before, they had to be now. But he kept his composure and offered her a slight smile in return. "Thanks. How similar is it to what you looked like ... you know ... before?"

"Would you like to see?"

"Sure. Have a photo in your wallet?"

She laughed. "No. But I was on Facebook. I have a ton of photos I can send."

She called upon her virtual assistant and instructed it to send a photo to Rajeev. Daniel popped up in Rajeev's field of vision a moment later. "I have a photo for you from Natalie Parsons," he said.

"Let's see it," Rajeev said.

The image appeared in front of him, showing a young, mousy, bespectacled woman with shoulder-length blond hair and a timid grin. Her eyes were blue and sparkled with the flash of the camera.

"How old are you in this photo?" Rajeev asked.

"Seventeen. It was just before my accident." She had already told Rajeev about how she'd dived into a pool, hit her head and damaged her spine, leaving her paralyzed. When she'd gotten the opportunity to be transferred into one of Next Level Technologies' robotic bodies, she'd been overjoyed. It was definitely a trade-off, but she'd considered it worth it. But then NLT had imprisoned her and she'd found herself trading one prison of a body for another.

But that had all changed. Rajeev had rescued her and now she was in a robotic body worlds better than the one she'd first been stuck in. When Rajeev had looked into the eyes of those original NLT bodies, he'd sometimes found it difficult to remember that there was a human consciousness in there, staring back out at him. But now, sitting on this bed next to Natalie and looking into her bright blue eyes, he thought he could see her soul.

"Well, you looked lovely," he said. "You still do," he added quickly.

She looked up at him curiously. "How old are you?"

"Depends on how you measure it. If you go by my reactivation in this new body, I'm about a day old."

"Obviously that's not what I meant."

"I know. But even then, it's tricky. I was thirty-nine when I got in a car accident, and I was in a coma for fifteen years after that before Dev ... well, Greg Maltek, actually ... uploaded me into a new body. By that measure, I'd be fifty-four. So which is correct? See my dilemma?"

Natalie nodded. "I do. That *is* a tricky situation."

"How old are you?"

"Twenty-three. And my situation is more straightforward. I was paralyzed for four years before I connected with NLT, and then I spent two years as their Guinea pig. It was so bad being stuck there that I was beginning to long for my pre-robot days—at least I wasn't anyone's slave back then."

"Well you're free now, and these bodies are a huge step up from the old ones. I almost feel human again, like I could go back to living something at least vaguely resembling my old life."

"Nothing will stay normal if Maltek gets his way," Natalie said gravely. "I swear, it's like I wake up from one nightmare just to find myself in another one."

"We'll end the nightmare," Rajeev said. "We'll end Maltek. We must."

Natalie shook her head slowly. "We're outnumbered. We're outgunned. He's been planning this for years. I'm ... I'm scared, Rajeev."

Rajeev nodded. The truth was, he was scared as well, but he couldn't give up hope.

"That's good," he said, and he placed a hand on her knee. "It means you're not stupid. But we'll outsmart him. We've got my son on our side. And he's a genius."

Natalie placed her hand on top of Rajeev's and looked into his eyes. Rajeev was dumbfounded by how human they looked. They were filled with a mixture of fear and longing as complex and rich as one would find in any human being's eyes. The engineers who had created these eyes had accomplished a feat that only God had accomplished before them, crafting windows into the soul.

She leaned forward and closed her eyes, cutting off those windows as she bridged the gap between she and Rajeev. But before it was bridged completely, the door opened and she quickly sat up as she and Rajeev turned to the door to see who had interrupted them. It was Dev.

He raised an eyebrow, sensing that he had walked in on something intimate, but he shook his head as if dismissing the awkwardness from the room. "Everyone's activated," he said. "It's time to train."

Ten

There was a space in the middle of the cavernous warehouse that was completely empty. It was supposed to be a space where the new equipment could be tested out, but now it was occupied by a circle of twelve androids—each of them in shiny new bodies—and one human, Dev, outfitted with one of the slim, new exoskeleton models. Mira had left to pick up her friends and bring them to the base, so Dev was the only representative of the legacy version of the human race.

"You're all aware that these bodies are far stronger than any human being," Dev said. "But Maltek's men are not ordinary human beings. They're strong, too. This is not a war that will be won with strength. It's a war that will be won with guile, cunning, and control. So it's essential that each of you becomes intimately familiar with how your body works and with the array of features included in it."

He walked into the center of the circle. "Who would like to volunteer?"

"Volunteer for what?" Ted asked.

"Just trust me," Dev said. "You can all handle it."

Brian, one of the androids Rajeev had gotten to know a bit back at Next Level Technologies, raised his hand. "I'll give it a go."

Dev motioned for him to step forward. In his new body, Brian towered over Dev, who was built rather like a marshmallow. Still, in his exoskeleton, there was no doubt Dev was formidable as well.

As if to demonstrate that very fact, Dev took a few long strides away from Brian, then turned around and motioned for him to come at him. "Let's see what you've got," he said.

"What, you want me to … attack you?" Brian asked.

"That's exactly what I want," Dev said. "Give me everything you've got."

Brian laughed, but Dev didn't, and Brian realized he was serious. He shrugged, took a step back, then shot at Dev as quickly as he could.

Dev dodged to the right, then swung his arm around and struck Brian in the back, sending him to the floor. The other androids laughed, but Dev quieted them. "This is exactly what I'm talking about. You all know you're powerful in your new bodies, but you don't know how to *use* those bodies. And that's what I'm going to teach you today. I helped design these models and I know them in and out. But before long, you'll know them even better than me, because you're actually *living in them*. We don't have time to wait for you to get used to the bodies on your own, however. We've gotta give you a crash course. Everyone find a partner."

Dev smiled as the androids paired up. It wasn't going to be easy, but they would build an army to match Maltek's. There was no way they would lose this war.

He wouldn't let them.

* * *

After nearly four hours of training, Dev called it a day—not for the androids' sake; they could have kept going all night. Rather, it was for his own sake. Although the exoskeleton increased his endurance significantly, he was still only human and his limits were far more evident than those of his robotic compatriots.

The androids had gathered around and were chattering excitedly among themselves. Dev thought they looked rather like soldiers commiserating after a long day of training. Of course, they were just getting started; there would be a lot more training to come.

"I have a treat for all of you," he said. He left, journeying into the rows of shelves as the androids craned their necks to see what he was doing, overwhelmed by curiosity. He returned a moment later carrying a large crate, which he placed on the ground in front of them.

"What's that?" one of them asked.

Dev reached into the crate and pulled out a small, white orb about the size of an apple. He tossed it to the android that had spoken.

"Put it up to your mouth."

He tentatively brought the orb near his mouth, and his eyes widened in response. "It's champagne!" he shouted.

The other androids began murmuring with a mix of confusion and excitement.

"Your new bodies are a huge improvement over the old ones, but unfortunately you're still not able to eat or drink," Dev said. "But you can still taste. These orbs use near-field wireless communication to approximate the tastes of various foods and beverages. This entire crate is filled with champagne-orbs. But don't indulge too much ... they also simulate drunkenness."

He passed the crate around and each of the androids plucked out an orb and brought it to their mouth. It didn't take long for the effects to kick in. Before long, they were laughing and talking like they had been best friends for years ... which is exactly what Dev had hoped for. If he wanted his army to behave as a cohesive unit, he needed soldiers that saw each other as brothers and sisters, as family. And the camaraderie he was now witnessing was a good start.

Eleven

Rajeev awoke the next morning with a hangover. When he realized what it was, he marveled: An honest-to-goodness hangover. He never thought he'd have one of those again.

Granted, it wasn't quite as bad as the kinds of hangovers real, flesh-and-blood people experienced. The orbs had been designed to interfere with the androids' thought processes to simulate the effects of alcohol, and there appeared to be residual effects on his faculties, making it somewhat difficult for him to think. Other than that, however, he was spared from many of the hangover symptoms he remembered from his life before he was a robot ... nausea, headaches, muscle soreness and the like.

He was lying in his bed in his dormitory, unsure of how he'd gotten there the previous night. He sat up, stretched his arms, then stood and made his way to the door.

Two card tables were set up in the open space where they'd trained yesterday. Seated around them were Dev, Mira, and the friends Mira had left to retrieve, including Zane, the engineering student who had helped Rajeev disable Next Level Technologies' failsafe the first time he'd escaped.

Seated beside Mira was Rosa, Mira's wife. And sitting across from them was Rajeev's ex-wife, Sarah. If he could even call her his ex, that is. Technically, since he was only a copy of the original Rajeev Sundaram, they had never actually been married. Still, the feelings and emotional attachments were there, which made it all the more painful to see the man sitting beside her with an arm wrapped around her shoulder.

"How'd you sleep, dad?" Dev walked up behind his dad and placed a hand on his shoulder.

"Not well enough."

"Here," Dev said, handing Rajeev an orb similar to the previous night's champagne.

Rajeev groaned. "Please, no," he said.

Dev laughed. "It's not more champagne, dad. It's coffee. Try it."

He brought the orb up to his mouth and felt a bitter yet pleasant sensation, followed by a surge of energy.

"Not bad," he said. "But couldn't you have programmed us in a way that would make hangovers impossible?"

"It's those kinds of familiar touches that make you feel like you're still human," Dev said. "You can't put a price on your humanity."

As Rajeev took a seat, he noticed Sarah's eyes on him. He looked different than he had before he was a robot, but she had recognized his voice as he'd spoken with Dev.

"Hello, Rajeev," she said, almost reverently.

"Hi, Sarah," he said. "It's good to see you." He turned to her companion. "And you are ...?"

Sarah shook her head. "Forgive me. Rajeev, this is Paul." Paul reached across the table and extended his hand to Rajeev. As they shook hands, he said, "I'm Sarah's husband."

So there it was. The final confirmation that Sarah had moved on—that she was, indeed, no longer his. But he'd known it all along, of course.

"Pleased to meet you, Paul," Rajeev said, trying to sound more pleasant and less emotional than he felt.

"I hope it's not awkward that I'm here," he said. "I mean, I know who you are and about your ... your past with Sarah ..."

"No," Rajeev lied. "No awkwardness. Like I said, it truly is a pleasure to meet you, Paul … as long as you've been taking care of her."

Sarah smiled and turned to look at her new husband affectionately. "He is," she said.

"This all must seem strange for both of you," Rajeev said, eager to change the subject.

"That's the understatement of the century," Paul said. "We were minding our own business when all of a sudden I find out my wife's ex is back from the dead, and a robot no less—no offense—and that a crazed tech entrepreneur has turned into a wannabe dictator. Now we're at war? It's insane."

Rajeev decided he rather liked Paul, even if he had more or less stolen his wife.

"No offense taken," he said. "And trust me, this is a war I would rather not fight. But Maltek hasn't really given us a choice."

"I just wish Paul and I could help," Sarah said.

Mira, who up until now had been silent, spoke up. "You guys can help," she said.

Sarah raised an eyebrow. "How?"

Rajeev smiled. "No one's shown you guys the exoskeletons yet?" They shook their heads, and Rajeev turned to Dev. "Looks like they're in need of a demonstration."

* * *

After Dev demonstrated how the exoskeletons worked, he got Sarah, Paul and the rest of Mira's friends outfitted with exoskeletons of their own. Their army was growing, but Rajeev still felt like they were woefully outmatched by the army Maltek had been secretly growing for years. He took Dev aside to share those concerns.

"We can only do what we can do," Dev replied unhelpfully.

"Of course," Rajeev said. "But that's exactly the point. We can do more."

"What are you proposing?"

"We need to grow our numbers. I mean, much more than we have been. Maltek has, what ... thousands of soldiers? Tens of thousands? Plus he's infiltrated the freakin' military."

"You're not wrong, but there's only so much we can do."

"We have to do more. We have to find a way. Couldn't we infiltrate the military, root out Maltek's spies?"

Dev put his hands to his face. "Maybe," he said. "I don't know how we'd go about doing it, but it could be worth a shot."

"We need to take every shot we've got if we want to win this war," Rajeev said.

Twelve

They received word from President Hollis that they were ready to move on Fresh Meat's headquarters in San Francisco. It was obviously too far to fly with their bodies' built-in flight capabilities, but thankfully, Dev had something in his underground hangar for just such an occasion: A supersonic jet.

Leaving Mira and the friends she'd brought to continue training at the compound, Dev and Rajeev led the rest of the androids onto the plane to head to San Francisco.

"So, this plane is underground," Rajeev said as they walked aboard. "How the hell are you going to get it airborne?"

"Remember, this was a military facility," Dev said. "It's filled with some pretty impressive tech." He sat down in the cockpit and explained to his father that flying the plane was all automated; he just had to input the destination and the plane would do the rest. After he did so, the ceiling in front of the plane parted and the sunlight streaming through revealed a long ramp ... a runway.

The engines roared to life and the jet began rolling across the runway, picking up speed until it was soaring through the air, headed to San Francisco. It continued building speed until it broke the sound barrier; the resulting supersonic boom thundered through the air around them.

"It won't take long to get there at this speed," Dev said.

"You don't really think we're going to find anything there, do you?"

Rajeev asked. "I'm sure Maltek picked up and left before his coup attempt."

"Probably not," Dev said. "But even the most carefully laid plans have gaps in them, and it's possible Maltek left behind some clue that will give us a better idea of what he's up to and how we can stop him. It's not likely, but I think it's certainly worth a look."

When they arrived in San Francisco, a group of government officials were waiting for them on the tarmac. A fastidiously groomed woman in a charcoal grey pantsuit approached Dev and held out her hand. "Hello Mr. Sundaram," she said. "I'm Agent Maxine Rathburn, FBI."

"Pleased to meet you, Ms. Rathburn," Dev said. "Anything we can do to help, just let us know."

She nodded. "For now, we just need you to accompany us in case Maltek decides to ambush us."

Rathburn ushered the group into a pair of black SUVs, and the caravan headed for Fresh Meat's headquarters.

They arrived at a building that, to a casual observer, would have seemed more or less unremarkable, its considerable height notwith-standing. But the entrance on the ground floor had been cordoned off with yellow police tape, and the area was swarming with law enforce-ment officials representing at least half a dozen different jurisdictions and agencies.

"Wait here," Rathburn told them as they got out of their vehicles. She walked up to a middle-aged man with a bald head and a protruding gut, then turned around and addressed the entire gathering.

"Listen up, people!" she shouted. "We're going in! Keep your eyes open for evidence, booby traps, anything—we don't know what we're going to encounter in here, so stay alert!"

A swarm of law enforcement officials entered the building first, most of them storming in with guns in their hands. The androids took up the rear.

Their footsteps echoed off the walls, and the way the sound bounced through the cavernous building left little doubt in Rajeev's mind that the building had been completely emptied out. As they made their way deeper inside, his suspicion was confirmed. Every room had been emptied of anything of importance. There were still desks and chairs, but any kind of computer equipment or electronic devices had been removed and taken who knows where.

Rajeev sidled up next to his son. "Looks like a graveyard," he muttered, softly enough that no one else would hear.

They scoured the building, but as far as Rajeev observed, nobody uncovered anything of significance. As everyone started packing up and heading out of the building, Rajeev and Dev conferred with Rathburn to see if her team had uncovered anything.

"Nothing terribly useful," she said. "Some random odds and ends that we'll analyze for fingerprints, but other than that I'm afraid we've come up empty-handed."

"In that case, I guess we'll have to wait for Maltek to make the first move," Rajeev said. "Which is unfortunate."

"That's a hell of an understatement," Dev said.

Thirteen

Rajeev was in poor spirits on the flight back. He felt helpless. They should be out doing something to track Maltek down, but there was nothing they *could* do. They had run into nothing but dead ends. As hopeful as he was that they'd eventually put a stop to Maltek's plans, he didn't think it was going to happen anytime soon. But when he expressed those sentiments to Dev, his son pushed back.

"We can't just sit around and do nothing, waiting for Maltek to strike," he insisted.

"I'm not proposing we sit around and do nothing. What I'm proposing is that we keep training so when Maltek does strike again, we can handle him and his soldiers."

"Soldiers?"

Rajeev nodded. "Let's be real about what they are." He paused and looked out the window. It was cloudy and he couldn't see the ground below, but the way the clouds soared past his line of sight was hypnotizing. When he spoke again, his words seemed more far away than they had before. "We need to grow our numbers," he said. "We need people stationed throughout the country so when Maltek strikes we have people there ready to go *immediately*. The next time he attacks, we might not get there soon enough to stop it." He looked up at his son. "Have you given any more thought to how we might get the military back on our side?"

"I'm still thinking about it. But I think I might have a temporary solution to the problem you just described. A way we could be in multiple places at once. It's not a perfect solution, but it's better than nothing."

"How is that possible?"

Dev flashed a crooked smile. "You're inhabiting a robotic body, yet you're questioning the wonders available to us thanks to modern technology? You should know better, dad. I'll show you when we get back to the base."

* * *

When they arrived back at the base, Dev led his father into the warehouse and to a shelf that was lined with what he had taken to calling "blanks"—bodies just like the one Rajeev was in, except they hadn't yet had a conscious mind downloaded into them.

"Help me carry it into my office," Dev said. He took the arms while Rajeev took the legs and they carried the body across the warehouse, both of them feeling like they were disposing of a corpse.

When they got to Dev's office, they set the body into a chair. It sat there, vacantly staring at them like a ventriloquist's dummy. Rajeev bent down and looked it straight in its dead eyes.

"It's weird seeing one that's … empty," he said.

"It won't be empty for long," Dev said. He flipped a switch on the side of the neck. "Turning on wireless communication," he explained. He sat down at his desk and got to work. After a moment, the body stood up straight as if it had come to life, and scared Rajeev half to death.

"It's alive?"

"No. It's essentially a drone. It just needs a pilot. Call up Daniel, would you?"

"What? Why?"

"Trust me, dad. Haven't you learned by now that I answer your questions by *showing* you the answers?"

Rajeev acquiesced and summoned his virtual assistant.

"What can I do for you?" Daniel asked.

"I don't know," Rajeev said, nodding to his son. "Ask him."

Daniel turned to Dev, looking at him quizzically.

"Daniel," Dev said, "initiate a neural link between Rajeev and that body there." He pointed to the body sitting in the chair. "By the way, dad, you'll want to sit down."

"What?"

"Just do it. Quickly."

Rajeev lowered himself onto the floor. As soon as he did so, Daniel initiated the link. Rajeev's body went limp, and the body on the chair sat up, startled.

"What's going on?" the body on the chair said.

"You're remotely controlling the body," Dev said. "Go ahead. Stand up. Move around a little."

Rajeev stood and took a few small, tentative steps forward in his new body. He seemed completely disoriented. "I'm controlling the other body?"

"Yes. Your mind is still attached, as it were, to the first body. But you're able to remotely control the other one. It's kind of like virtual reality, except you're controlling a physical body that exists in the real world."

"It's weird," Rajeev said, turning his hands back and forth in front of his eyes.

"You'll get used to it, just like you got used to each of your other robotic bodies," Dev said. "But you see the utility of this, don't you? We can place these empty vessels with allies across the country. That way, no matter where Maltek strikes, you or one of the other androids can instantly take control of one of these bodies and be ready to fight."

Rajeev nodded. "It's not perfect, but it could work," he said. "How soon can we get these shipped out?”

"I'll start preparing them for shipment immediately."

Fourteen

Gregory Maltek was restless. He was frustrated. But, more than anything, he was angry.

He hadn't anticipated Dev Sundaram and his android freaks confronting him the way they had at the White House. He should have taken over by now. It should have been a done deal.

But he shouldn't be so naive. Dev hadn't stopped him. He'd merely set him back. He was still coming for the government, and for Dev. His rise was inevitable. He'd just have to work a little harder to get there than he'd anticipated.

Which is exactly what he was doing now: Working to achieve his ultimate goal. He hadn't had any intention of becoming a terrorist, but it seemed he had to send Dev a message, to make it clear just how high the stakes were. Dev needed to understand that there was nothing Gregory Maltek wouldn't do to take control of this country and every person in it so he could bring his grand vision of the future to life. And he wouldn't stop there. He would take control of the United States, and then he would take control of the world. With the entire globe under his thumb, there would be no more need for war or conflict, for politics or for espionage.

A tall, muscular, bald man dressed in combat gear approached Maltek. "We're just about ready, boss. Just waiting for your go-ahead."

Maltek took a deep breath. The corner of his lips turned up in a slight smile. He faced the man and nodded.

"Go ahead," he said. "Do it."

* * *

Dev and Rajeev were meeting in Dev's office when the breaking news alert came up via their virtual assistants. For Rajeev, it took the form of a hovering headline scrolling across his field of vision: "EXPLOSION DESTROYS SEATTLE SPACE NEEDLE: TERRORISM SUSPECTED, SAY POLICE."

Dev and Rajeev locked eyes. "Maltek?" Rajeev asked.

Dev nodded. "Looks like it's time to test out our remote response plan."

"Do we have bodies in Seattle yet?"

"Yes, thank God. Come on; let's gather the team."

When they stepped out of the office, the rest of their growing team was staring into space, obviously watching coverage of the Space Needle explosion. It wasn't clear if they realized it was Maltek's work. Rajeev wasn't quite as sure that it was Maltek as Dev was, but he suspected his son's instinct was right. Either way, it was prudent for them to respond; better safe than sorry.

"Let's go, guys," Dev said, his voice echoing through the cavernous warehouse. "We're heading to Seattle."

Mira snapped out of her reverie, muttering under her breath for her virtual assistant to stop playing the news coverage of the explosion. "You think this was Maltek?"

"I wouldn't be surprised," Dev said. "We need to assume it is until we know otherwise."

They lined up against the wall near Dev's office and sat down, their backs resting against the wall, awaiting further instructions from Dev.

"One of us should hang back and guard the others," he said. "Otherwise we're all sitting ducks if someone manages to infiltrate our base. I don't think that's likely, but we should be prepared for the possibility."

"I'll do it," Zane said.

Dev nodded. "Thanks, Zane. As for the rest of you, a quick refresher: Pull up your virtual assistant, then ask them to initiate a neural link with your analogue in Seattle. Make sure you mention the city so they know which body specifically to link you to."

He observed as they initiated the links, making sure that none of them had any problems. When they were all successfully linked, he sat his back against the wall and called upon his own virtual assistant. Controlling the bodies wasn't quite as immersive an experience for humans as it was for the androids, who had digitized minds that could easily be transferred to other bodies. But it worked well enough, and under the circumstances, it was better than nothing.

They awoke in a small, nondescript office. None of them were sure exactly where they were in the city; they'd worked with President Hollis' administration to place the bodies throughout the country, so they weren't involved in picking the exact locations. It didn't matter, though; their virtual assistants could navigate them to where they needed to be.

Dev was the last to awaken and found that everyone else was standing and ready to go. He rose to his feet and nodded toward the door. "Everyone ready to go?"

He led them out and asked his assistant to take them to the Space Needle. A map appeared in front of his eyes with a route plan and a time estimate: Twenty minutes.

"Twenty minutes isn't fast enough," he said. "Let's fly; we should be able to get there in five."

One by one, they instructed their voice assistants to fly them to their destination, and they took off into the air.

Less than five minutes later, they landed on a patch of grass next to the Space Needle ... or at least, next to what used to be the Space Needle. The rubble of what had been the famous tourist destination was still burning; if they hadn't been in bodies constructed of heat-resistant materials, they wouldn't have been able to stand as close to the wreckage as they were. Thankfully, their bodies allowed them to stand directly on the smoldering debris without any detrimental effects. Unfortunately, it was clear that anyone who had happened to be inside the structure at the time of the explosion had not survived.

Rajeev walked over the wreckage slowly, reverently. He thought he spotted a severed hand, but he turned his head before he could confirm the identity of the object. He felt like he was going to be sick. This truly was a war, and these were the first civilian casualties. *No*, Rajeev told himself, *this, here, isn't warfare. It's terrorism.*

"I can't be here," he said. The only one within earshot was Dev.

"We have to be here. If not us, who?"

Rajeev had no words. Just as he was about to formulate a response, he was interrupted by a clamor on the far side of the wreckage. All of the androids turned at once toward the noise. They saw nothing at first; then, some of the rubble began to move. Something was stirring beneath the surface. As it emerged, the debris rose and fell off it. At the same time, half a dozen other objects began rising, encircling the androids and leaving them no means of escape.

With the first object now fully uncovered, they could see what they were looking at: a giant exoskeleton, like the one Rajeev had used to rescue the other androids from the NLT campus, only bigger. As the other objects fully emerged, it became clear that they, also, were oversized versions of the exoskeletons that Dev had designed.

The first exoskeleton took a step forward and raised an arm, as if it were preparing to recite poetry.

"Welcome, Dev." It was Maltek's voice. "I've been expecting you."

Fifteen

Dev rushed forward, and when Rajeev realized that he meant to attack Maltek, he headed him off and held him back.

"Why did you do this?" Dev spat. "There were innocent people in there! You're a monster!"

Maltek chuckled, and the sound was so enraging that Rajeev almost let go of his son so he could take a swipe at him—but, of course, if he were to let him go he'd merely be destroyed by Maltek's giant exoskeleton.

"Me?" Maltek asked with false indignation. "I didn't do this, Dev. *You* did. If you hadn't felt the need to challenge me, to fight against the inevitable, then this little display of power wouldn't have been necessary. But you couldn't leave well enough alone, could you? You had to rebel against me like a petulant teenager, and now you must live with the consequences of your actions."

"That's some twisted logic," Dev spat.

"You don't have to understand it," Maltek retorted. "You just have to live by it. You can't stop me. I'm going to change the world—for the *better*. You can fight it—and cause innumerable deaths just like the ones that lay beneath our feet—or you can accept it, and even join me. Think of what the two of us could accomplish together. Two brilliant minds like ours? The possibilities are endless."

"I'll never help you."

There was a pause, as if Maltek was punishing Dev with his silence, like a disappointed parent. When he spoke again, his voice was cold, empty of the sarcastic tone that had heretofore punctuated his speech.

"Then you'll need to get out of my way. And if you refuse to do so willingly, as appears to be the case, I'll force you."

As if on cue, one of the androids collapsed, as if he'd suddenly lost consciousness. The androids looked down at their fallen comrade, then up at each other. And then it happened again—to Brian this time. One moment he was looking into the eyes of his compatriots in fearful confusion; the next, he was laying on the ground in a lifeless heap.

Dev looked up at Rajeev, his eyes filled with abject terror. "What's going on?"

Rajeev offered a helpless shrug. "I don't know." He tried to sound nonchalant, but on the inside he was as terrified as Dev.

When the third android dropped, Dev began to piece together what was going on. "Something's happening back at the base!" he shouted to the others. "A malfunction or ... something. I'm not sure if it's Maltek or something else, but we should all log off."

Mira scoffed. "But what about Maltek?"

"There's nothing we can do about him now," Dev said. "We're outmatched. Everyone, retreat—log off and return to the base." As soon as he'd finished uttering the words, his artificial body collapsed—he'd logged off and there was no mind left to occupy it and keep it standing.

Rajeev followed suit. The transition was jarring; one moment he was in Seattle on top of the wreckage of the Space Needle; the next he was back at the base, seated on the floor against the wall. It took his eyes a moment to adjust, but when they did he was presented with the sight of Dev and Zane, their arms locked as they wrestled each other.

"What the hell is going on?" Rajeev shouted.

Dev spoke through gritted teeth as he continued to fight Zane. "He's working for Maltek!"

Rajeev's eyes drifted over to the other androids. They were all back now and were standing, except for three of them—the three who had collapsed in Seattle. It appeared their heads had been bashed at the base, and Rajeev realized what his son had just said must be true: Zane, the man who was supposed to be watching over them, protecting them, was actually a double agent working for their enemy. He leapt forward and approached Zane from behind. He wrapped his arms around his neck and pulled. Zane began to choke and sputter until, finally, he lost consciousness and went limp. Rajeev lowered him to the floor.

"What the hell?" Mira asked. "This is not like Zane. Not at all."

Dev was still catching his breath, but he answered his sister's query the best he could. "I don't think it's Zane," he said. "I think it's one of Maltek's clones."

"Just like the one he made of you," Rajeev said.

Dev nodded. "He created another spy for himself."

"Then where's the real Zane?" Mira asked.

"I'd hate to speculate," Dev said. "Best case scenario, he never knew they'd gotten ahold of his DNA and copied him."

Mira shook her head. "That can't be the case," she said. "When I went and got him, it was at his house. So if this imposter was there in Zane's house, and Zane wasn't ..." She trailed off.

"Then that means something bad happened to Zane," Rajeev said, finishing her sentence.

"There's nothing we can do about it now," Dev said. "Maybe we can get an answer out of him when he comes to, but I wouldn't count on it."

"Oh, I'll make *sure* we get it out of him," Rajeev said. Even as he said the words, he was surprised by them. It was out of character for him to threaten to torture someone as he just had. This war was changing him. It was changing all of them—and not for the better. But what choice did they have if they wanted to win?

"This represents a bigger problem," Dev said. "This is the second spy Maltek has sent into our midst. How do we know he doesn't already have another spy with us? How would we know if he sent one in?"

Natalie, who thus far had been silent, scanned the room. "Any one of us could be one of his spies," she said.

"We need to devise a test," Rajeev said. "A way to tell if someone's consciousness has been artificially implanted in their body. Is it possible, Dev?"

Dev sucked in air through his teeth. "Possible? Maybe. But it'll be difficult as hell to figure out, and it could take a long time—and time is a luxury we don't have."

"We don't have a choice," Rajeev said. "You'd better get started."

Sixteen

He killed Brian," Natalie said, standing over the fallen android. "And two of the others ... I never learned their names."

"They'll be okay," Dev said. "All three of their minds are backed up. I can restore them. But if he'd gotten to me, or Mira ... or mom or Paul ... there would be no coming back from that."

"You don't have *their* minds backed up?"

Dev paused. "Well, I do, but ..."

"But the duplicates aren't as good as the real thing."

"I didn't say that."

"You didn't have to."

He sighed. "I didn't mean anything by it. Yes, the minds could have been restored, but if we'd lost our bodies ... I realize these artificial ones can do some pretty amazing things, but I think you understand why we are so attached to the bodies we were born with."

Her face softened. "You're right," she said. "I'm sorry."

"Let's leave Dev alone to work on a solution to our spy problem," Rajeev said. Natalie nodded and Rajeev led her away so Dev could retire to his office to work.

"You seemed pretty upset," Rajeev said. They entered his dorm and Natalie followed him in.

"I'm sorry about that. I couldn't help getting emotional." She grinned. "I'm not a robot, you know ... as much as I may look like it on the outside."

"Well, it's a good thing you're a robot on the outside. It gives you a second chance if something happens to you."

"It almost seems like cheating, doesn't it?"

"You've gotta take the pros where you find them. There are plenty of cons."

They each took a seat on Rajeev's bed. Rajeev felt exhausted—more mentally than physically—and he got the sense that Natalie was, too. It was dawning on both of them what it really meant to be at war—especially a war in which they were vastly outmatched by their enemy. Dev had backed up their minds, so death wasn't quite as much of a concern as it would be for a typical soldier. But even so ... what if Maltek killed Dev? What if he found their base, blew it up, and destroyed the backups? Then they would truly be gone from this earth. They would truly be casualties of war.

"Are you scared?" Natalie asked. It took Rajeev aback—it was like she'd been reading his mind.

"I don't think I should be," he said, "but I can't help but be a little scared. I don't think it's entirely for my own sake. I'm scared for the world, and everyone in it, and what will happen to them if Maltek wins."

Natalie nodded her head solemnly. "Maybe it's selfish of me, but I'm just scared for myself. I don't want to die. I know that my mind is backed up, that I can come back, in a way ... but what if that copy isn't really *me*?"

Rajeev wasn't sure he should say anything, but he couldn't help himself. "You know, you've already been through this once before ... when they put you into your first robotic body."

She nodded. "I've thought about that ... about how, in a sense, the woman who came before is gone. But I'm here now, whatever I am, and I don't want to be gone, regardless of whatever comes after me."

He nodded. "Yeah, I agree. But we can't let our fear paralyze us."

Natalie looked up at Rajeev's face, and as she spoke, there was a new determination in her eyes. "We won't," she said.

The door swung open; it was Mira, and she barely looked at them before speaking and heading back out.

"Faux-Zane is awake," she said. "Come on; we've got questions, and he's going to give us the answers."

Seventeen

Faux-Zane was tied to a chair near Dev's office. Sweat had formed on his forehead, but he otherwise seemed calm. Dev emerged from his office and regarded the captive with barely concealed rage.

"Shouldn't you be working?" Rajeev asked.

Dev shook his head. "I could use the break. And this is more important for now, anyway."

He walked directly up to Zane, then crouched so they were face-to-face. He tapped the side of his head, then slightly tilted his own.

"Who is that inside there?" he asked. "Is that you, Maltek? Or are you just one of his lackeys?"

Zane returned Dev's stare, but remained defiantly silent. Rajeev could see that his refusal to talk was frustrating Dev.

"What did you do with the real Zane?"

"I am the real Zane."

"Bullshit!" Dev's face was red now, and he had dropped all pretense of politeness. "The real Zane wouldn't have murdered his own allies."

The imposter's face grew hard, and he said nothing more. Dev stared him down for a long minute, but it was fruitless. Out of nowhere, he pulled back his fist, then brought it down on Zane's right cheek.

His fist bounced back as if he'd punched a steel door. He covered his hurt fist with the other one and recoiled in pain.

"Son of a bitch!"

Zane grinned. "Guess you forgot that Maltek's creating supermen."

Dev frowned. He stared Zane down, then spoke in a low, menacing voice.

"I guess you forgot that I am as well." He nodded toward his father. "Show him how serious we are."

Rajeev hesitated. He wanted answers as much as Dev did, but he didn't want to get them this way.

"Dev, I ... I can't."

Dev didn't look pleased with his father's disobedience, even if it was a matter of conscience. He was about to argue, but then Natalie stepped up so he didn't have to.

"I'll do it," she said. She walked up to the bound man and stared at him with genuine hatred. He was a wolf in a sheep pen, and that meant he was someone to be both feared and reviled. She struck him in the face and unlike Dev, she did not recoil in pain. Zane's head snapped back and when he looked up at Natalie afterward, he didn't look as cocky as he had a moment before. Dev and Rajeev shared a look. Who knew Natalie had *this* in her?

"Where is Zane?" she asked.

"Screw you."

She hit him again, even harder this time. But instead of waiting for a response, she hit him again, in the chest, and his chair fell back onto the ground with a loud clang. Natalie stooped down next to him and placed a hand on his throat. "Where is he?" He didn't answer, so she increased the pressure on his throat and asked again: "*Where is he?*"

"He's fine!" Faux-Zane finally sputtered. "He's alive! Lay off!"

She removed her hand from his throat, but she didn't pull the chair back up. She inched her face up to his. "Where is he? Where can we find him?"

"I don't know."

She stood and raised her foot above his crotch. Before she could bring it down, he cried out.

"Maltek has him," he said. "The original Maltek. He's safe, unharmed, but detained."

"Where is Maltek?" she asked.

"I don't know."

"Bullshit," she said, and began lowering her foot, but he stopped her.

"Honestly, I don't know! Maltek never told me, for this exact reason. He didn't want me giving away his location."

"You'd better tell us something we can use or you're dead meat," Natalie growled.

"Nothing I say will save you," he said. "You're screwed no matter what. Maltek is a step ahead of you. He will always be a step ahead of you."

Natalie bent down and placed her hand back on his throat. She began to squeeze, and the look in her eyes made it apparent she had no intention of stopping until he was dead.

"Stop!" Dev shouted. He ran over to them and pulled Natalie back. "We need him alive."

"He's not going to tell us shit. Let's be done with him!"

"We need him to test the device I'll hopefully be able to create. If you want to be able to differentiate between us and spies, we *need* him. Keep him alive."

Natalie glared at him, but she backed off. "What are we going to do with him?"

"Lock him in one of the dorms," Dev said. "Tie him to the bed, lock the door, and keep two guards posted outside."

Natalie nodded. She gathered two other androids and they lifted Faux-Zane, chair and all, and carried him off toward the dorms.

Rajeev turned to his son. His exhaustion was evident in his voice.

"What do we do now?"

"Get some rest, dad," Dev said, as he headed back to his office. "I have a lot of work to do, very quickly."

Eighteen

H ow's it going?" Rajeev asked, walking into Dev's office.

Dev was bent over a workbench at the far side of the office. It was filled with equipment—wires, soldering irons, scraps of metal, and a variety of other tech Rajeev didn't recognize. He took a step back and wiped his brow.

"I'm close. In fact, I think I'll have a working prototype before too long."

"That's great. I had another idea that may help us as well."

"Yeah? Let's hear it."

"We need to know what our little Zane imposter knows, right? We need to get inside his head. And it just so happens that getting in people's heads is your specialty."

Dev nodded. "You want me to scan him. Duplicate his mind."

"Why wouldn't you?"

"It's a little unethical to scan someone's brain without their consent."

Rajeev scoffed. "Hello—you never asked for my consent!"

"That was different. It was personal. Besides, I've already apologized for that, dad."

"And I appreciate that. But this is war, Dev. We need to do whatever it takes to win. Right now we're outgunned and, loathe as I am to admit it, that imposter out there was right—Maltek is several steps ahead of us. This may be our only chance to get back in the game."

Dev sighed. "You're right. In fact, having a scan of his brain could help me finish this device. Let's do it right now."

* * *

Rajeev had not yet seen what the process of mapping out and duplicating a mind looked like, even though he had gone through that very process. Dev had retrieved a bowl-shaped device, a laptop computer, and a pile of wires and cords, then made for the dorm where Faux-Zane was being held captive, with Rajeev in tow.

Zane was strapped to the bed, just as Dev had ordered. As the pair entered the room, he attempted to look up to see who had come in, but couldn't until Dev sat his equipment down and stood over him.

"Finally come to let me go?" he asked sarcastically.

Dev ignored him. He placed the bowl on top of Zane's head, securing it with a strap that wrapped around his chin. As he did so, Zane wriggled around and became visibly concerned.

"What are you doing?" he asked, rolling his head around in an attempt to prevent Dev from doing ... whatever he was doing. Dev, however, didn't feel inclined to offer an explanation.

"Stay still," he barked. With the headpiece secured, he plugged two cords into it, then connected them to the laptop. He opened it and began typing, setting up parameters Rajeev could only guess at.

Zane turned his head toward Dev. "You're going to scan my brain?" Rajeev couldn't be sure, but he thought he detected a hint of panic in the imposter's voice. And if scanning his mind made him nervous, then Rajeev was confident it was the correct course of action.

Dev ignored him, and after a moment the headpiece began emitting a faint blue glow and a low scanning noise. Dev set the laptop on the ground and stood. "Now we wait," he said.

"How long?" Rajeev asked.

"It varies. It could take anywhere from five to twelve hours."

"Wow."

Dev shrugged. "Considering the complexity of the human brain, I don't think it's really that long to wait."

"That's probably true. But what are we going to do for five hours or longer?"

"All we can do ... wait."

Nineteen

Faux-Zane had settled down after realizing there was nothing he could do to stop his brain scan. But when Rajeev and Dev reentered the room seven hours later, he didn't look happy about it.

"Looks like it's done," Dev said. He removed the headpiece, picked up the laptop, and headed out of the room with his father.

"Hey, wait," Zane called out, a hint of panic in his voice. "Aren't you going to unrestrain me?"

Dev stopped and gave Zane what Rajeev could only describe as a death stare. "You're lucky we haven't killed you yet, you traitorous little son of a bitch. The only reason you're strapped to that bed and not buried in the ground is because you're useful to us. So be grateful you're restrained. You wouldn't like the alternative."

He turned and walked out with Zane's eyes burning into him the entire time. Rajeev couldn't quite tell if the prisoner was watching him with fear, awe, or even respect in his eyes ... or perhaps a combination of all three.

Rajeev ran out of the room and caught up to his son. "You didn't really mean that, did you?"

Dev shrugged. He looked rattled. "Maybe. Maybe not. I honestly don't know."

"I know he's a spy, but he's a human being."

"Yeah. And we're at war. And human beings like that won't hesitate to kill us or deliver information that will lead to our deaths. It might sound callous, but better him than me. Better him than you, or mom, or Mira, or any of us. I don't know what I'm going to do with him, but if I feel the only way to truly neutralize any threat he may pose is to take him out ... well, I might hesitate, but only for a moment."

Dev led Rajeev into his office and motioned for him to take a seat as he worked on the laptop. He pulled up a 3D image of a brain and pointed to it.

"This is Zane's brainscan," he said.

Rajeev stood and came in for a closer look. "That's it? That's the sum total of the person occupying his mind?"

Dev nodded. "It's a much more straightforward procedure than it was for you. Since you'd been in an accident and suffered brain damage, we had to fill in the gaps with publicly available data. Zane here, thankfully, has not suffered any such brain trauma and as such, his mind is a perfect specimen for duplication. This is just a graphical representation of the scan. Here's what the raw data looks like." He pressed a button and the screen changed to reveal a never-ending string of code that was completely indecipherable to Rajeev.

"You can read that?"

Dev shook his head. "No, but the program can read the code and display it as the graphical representation we were just looking at. It can also display the data like this ..." with a few quick presses of the keyboard, the screen changed again, this time displaying a small, 3D humanoid figure. It was round and featureless, its skin pale white. It looked like a crude sculpture of a human being that had recently been cured and not yet been painted.

"What is that thing?" Rajeev asked.

"This is Zane's consciousness. With a few modifications. Since we have a full map of Zane's brain we can also modify it as we like. So we can manipulate his consciousness such that it becomes an open book—no defensiveness, no malice, no ulterior motives. It's as if we've given him a truth serum."

"That's terrifying. And to think that people were concerned about their privacy on social media."

"It's definitely a huge responsibility to have access to this information, and normally this isn't something I would ever do. But in this case, it's necessary."

"I understand. Still find it creepy, though. So what are you going to ask it?"

Dev leaned forward as if the tiny figure on the screen needed help hearing him. "What is your name?"

A monotone, robotic voice came through the laptop's speakers. "Gregory Maltek."

Dev turned to his father. "No surprise there. He duplicated his own consciousness and downloaded it into a clone of Zane. What an egomaniac ... he can't delegate anything; he's got to make copies of himself to do his bidding." He turned back to the computer screen. "Where are you hiding out, Gregory? Not the copy of you that was uploaded into Zane's clone, but the original Gregory Maltek?"

The figure shook its head. "I don't know."

"How can it not know?" Rajeev asked.

"Maltek must have anticipated that we'd try scanning the clone's brain. He could have found some way to delete some of the information, block access to certain memories."

Rajeev turned to the screen. "Where is the real Zane?" he asked.

"He's being detained," the figure said.

"Where?"

"I don't know."

Rajeev let out a frustrated sigh. "We're not getting anywhere," he said.

"We're not, but I think we're coming at it too directly. We need to come at it from the side, poke at information Maltek wouldn't have thought to obscure. He's made it difficult for us, but it's not impossible."

"I'll defer to you. I have no idea what to ask it."

Dev thought a moment. When he spoke, his voice was hesitant, uncertain. "What motivates you, Gregory? Why are you building an army?"

"To create a better world."

Dev looked up at Rajeev and frowned. He turned back to the tiny figure. "What do you mean?" he asked. "Elaborate."

"Humanity is chaotic," it said. "Chaos leads to greed, to fights, to wars. Chaos leads to death. The antidote to chaos is control—and control is a commodity I can provide."

"Dear Lord," Rajeev said. "He really believes this, doesn't he?"

"He must," Dev answered. "The way I've configured the program, there's no capacity to lie. He may have delusions of grandeur, but they're sincere delusions." He turned back to the figure on the screen. "How do you intend to accomplish that goal?"

"I'll provide everyone on the planet one of our proprietary bodies," it said. "Once that's accomplished, we can eradicate all of the world's ills. We can program the bodies to make them incapable of committing violence, incapable of committing theft, incapable of telling a lie. I will create a perfect paradise inhabited by a perfect populace."

"He wants to enslave humanity," Dev said.

Rajeev nodded. "He's a madman. But that was already obvious."

Dev turned his attention back to the avatar. "How would you go about implementing that? How would you force people into your bodies?"

"I'll take over the federal government. Once we have control, we'll use the might of the military to force people into my products."

"And what if you try to take over and fail? What if, for whatever reason, someone stops you?"

The figure paused for a few seconds before answering, as if it were contemplating an answer to the question. "Then we'll move south," it said. "We'll go down the line until we succeed and then we'll circle back around and tie up any loose ends."

Dev ended the program and the figure disappeared. He stood and began walking out of the room.

"That's it?" Rajeev asked, following his son out the door. "You're done with him? What are you going to do with Faux-Zane?"

"Nothing, for now. We'll deal with him later. We have more pressing matters to deal with now."

"Like what?"

Dev turned and looked his father straight in the face. "We have to go to Mexico," he said.

Twenty

Rajeev hadn't seen Dev's logic at first, but he'd eventually come around to his son's line of thinking. Maltek had said he would "move south." He'd already tried to overtake the U.S. government and failed. The next country down the line was Mexico. Where exactly would Maltek strike? They couldn't be sure, but the capital, of course, was Mexico City, so it made sense to start there.

"So, what are we going to do in Mexico, exactly?" Natalie asked. Dev had just finished laying out his case to the group.

"We're going to wait," Dev said. "We'll search the city and see if we can sniff him out, but more likely, he'll make a move against the government and we'll be there to stop him just like in D.C. But hopefully this time we'll be able to stop him for good."

Ted nodded. "Sounds good to me. When do we leave?"

Dev's lips turned up in a slight grin. "How fast can you pack?"

As everyone left to prepare for the trip, Rajeev turned to his son. He couldn't hide the concern on his face.

"What are we going to do with our ... prisoner?" he asked.

"I was avoiding having to deal with that. But I think there's only one thing we *can* do."

"You're going to kill him."

A pained look came over Dev's face. "It's not like I *want* to kill him. But he's a liability. He tried to kill us when we were in Seattle remotely, remember? If he were to get loose somehow, there's no doubt he wouldn't hesitate for a moment to harm any one of us, or to sell us out to Maltek—you know, the *original* Maltek. I don't see any other choice."

"There has to be another option than murder," Rajeev said, sounding like he was trying to convince himself as much as his son.

"There are many options, but I can't think of a better one. All the alternatives are too risky."

"So how do you plan to do it?"

"I'm open to suggestions."

Rajeev shook his head as if he couldn't believe they were discussing the matter. "Whatever is most humane, I guess. Do you have drugs here? Maybe you could do a 'lethal injection.'"

Dev nodded. "I'm sure I can put something together."

He led his father to a shelf lined with medical supplies. A moment later they were walking away, Dev's arms filled with the supplies he'd need to put a man to death

When they came to the door, Rajeev opened it and let his son pass through. Before he could follow him inside, he heard the clatter of his son dropping the supplies on the floor. He rushed inside to find Dev looking stunned, as if he'd just been struck in the face.

"What's wrong?"

Dev pointed at the bed, and Rajeev's eyes followed his son's outstretched finger to the source of his stunned silence.

The bed was empty.

Twenty-One

Whathat the hell?" Rajeev crouched and looked under the bed, recognizing as he did so how ridiculous he must look. "Where did he go?"

"He's gone," Dev said, stunned.

"But how?"

Dev's face grew dark. "He had help." He marched out of the room and called out to the team scattered throughout the warehouse. "Everyone outside my office *now!*" he bellowed.

He went inside his office, and when he emerged a moment later he was carrying a device that looked similar to the one he'd used to copy Faux-Zane's mind, and a crowd had dutifully formed just outside.

"This," he said, holding out the device, "is the device I built to detect spies. I'm going to subject each and every one of you to it, because we have a spy in our midst. We're going to root them out right now."

"What are you talking about?" Mira asked. "What makes you say there's a spy?"

"Zane is gone." Hushed whispers drowned him out, and Dev raised his hands to quiet them. "Someone let him go. Hence, my statement that there's a spy among us. Now let's get this out of the way. We have more important things to attend to."

He placed a chair from his office out in the open. Mira volunteered to go first. She took a seat and Dev strapped the device to her head. He hooked the device up to a laptop and initiated the scan.

It took more than ten minutes for the device to finish scanning her brain, but when it was complete, Dev was satisfied with the results. "She's clean," he said.

He went through the same process with everyone else in the group. The test was more limited for the androids; because their minds were all foreign to their bodies, they would all register as potential spies under the test, which was essentially a false positive. Dev was able to test the androids' minds against the scan of Faux-Zane, however, and confirm that none of them was a match for Maltek. It wasn't a perfect solution, but so far all the spies they'd actually uncovered had been copies of Maltek's mind, so Dev was fairly confident any android that passed the test was clean.

One by one, they all put on the machine and underwent the test—even Rajeev and Dev themselves—and they all came back clean.

"I don't understand it," Dev said, frustration dripping off his lips. "There *has* to be a spy. How else could Zane have escaped?"

"Is it possible he escaped by himself, without help?" Ted asked.

"I don't see how. He was strapped in pretty tightly."

"And yet it appears to be the most likely scenario based on the information we have at the moment," Rajeev said.

Dev brought his hands to his temples. "I don't see how he could have gotten out without help."

"Every single one of us just came back clean, and we need to get down to Mexico ASAP. I suggest we table this question for now and come back to it when the fate of the entire world isn't weighing on our shoulders."

Dev released a deep sigh. "Okay. You're right. Let's go." He looked up and raised his voice to address the entire group. "Finish packing," he said. "Let's get this show on the road."

* * *

With their supersonic jet, they were in Mexico in no time. For the humans, the weather was punishing; the sun beat down on their skin and within moments, they'd broken out into full sweats. The weather made no difference to the androids, however. Their artificial bodies were designed to withstand temperatures far more extreme than the Mexican heat.

Hollis had worked with the Mexican government to arrange for a place for them to stay—an old underground military bunker, similar to their headquarters back home, except that it was smaller, older, and decidedly less state-of-the-art.

There was less living space. Instead of individual dormitories, there were simply several lines of cots set up for them to sleep on. After everyone had claimed a cot and placed their belongings beneath it, they gathered around the entrance to receive further instructions from Dev.

Or, as Ted put it, "What the hell do we do now?"

"First things first," Dev said, "everyone needs to be on high alert. There's a decent chance Maltek will make a move before we find him and we need to be prepared to respond. But if we can find him first, that would be ideal. Better we catch him off guard than the other way around."

"What if we find him?" Ted asked.

"Then use your virtual assistant to call the rest of us, and we'll help you take him out. All of us are mere minutes away from each other with our built-in flight capabilities. Don't alert him to your presence if you can help it. Don't do anything stupid. Wait for backup, and we can make our move together." He looked around, making eye contact with the other members of the group. "Any other questions?" He waited a moment and when no one else spoke up, he nodded. "Good. Let's get out there and flush Maltek out like the rodent he is."

Twenty-Two

Everyone split up into groups of two to sweep the city. As it happened, Rajeev was paired up with Natalie.

He couldn't help but feel like an outsider as they traversed the streets; not just because they were foreigners, but also because they were robots walking among flesh-and-blood people. But their new bodies represented a vast improvement over the old models, and nobody seemed to notice that they weren't quite fully human.

As the day wore on, they found themselves coming up empty-handed. They'd shared a photograph of Maltek with everyone they came across, but nobody seemed to have seen him. As the sun began to set, they passed by a cantina and Natalie suggested they pop in.

"Aren't you forgetting something?" Rajeev asked. "We can't eat or drink. There's nothing for us in there."

Natalie flashed him a wry smile. "Now, now, Mr. Sundaram. There's more to life than food and drink." She shot him a bright smile, then marched inside without a backward glance to see if he was following her inside. But of course he was going to follow her—it's not like he could just leave her there.

As he walked in, he was surprised to find that she was already seated at a table, looking up at him expectantly. A band was situated in the corner of the restaurant, vigorously playing Mariachi music. As he sat down beside her, Natalie nodded in the band's direction.

"Isn't this cool?"

He shrugged. "I guess."

"Stop trying to act too cool for school," she said, hitting him lightly on the arm. "We're in a Mexican cantina experiencing a real, live Mariachi band. You'd never experience anything like this back in Chicago."

"You're right," he said, letting himself relax a bit and take in the sound of the music. "I wouldn't."

The cantina was populated with just enough patrons to generate a gentle murmur resonating just beneath the music. Rajeev watched a man take a long, deep drink of a pint of beer and he wished he had an icy glass for himself—or at least, one of the fake alcoholic orbs Next Level Technologies had developed to let androids feel halfway human. But he had to admit Natalie was right. He was enjoying himself even without food or drink. It was more than just the music; it was the entire ambiance of the place. The murmuring of the patrons lent an energy to the space that reminded him of one of the essential components of humanity that he'd started to forget: A broad sense of community.

"I admit it; this was a cool experience," Rajeev said as the band took a break between songs. "Thank you for insisting on coming here."

"Someone's got to push you out of your shell from time to time."

"Had you ever been to Mexico, you know ... before?"

She shook her head. "Never. You?"

"Once, when I was a teenager," he said. "It wasn't a very exciting trip. I was poor and came down with a few of my friends, mainly just to get drunk off cheap beer in a more exotic locale than our usual stomping grounds in Chicago."

"I like it here," Natalie said. "You can tell there's a slower pace of life here. Even in the midst of all this craziness—hunting Maltek, the fate of the world in our hands—I can tell people here take the time to relax and enjoy the things that really matter in life."

"The fate of the world really is in our hands, though. We should probably get back to it."

Her face fell, just a little. "Can't we just stay for one more song?"

He took in the earnest look in her eyes and couldn't help but sympathize. Their lives had been thrust into nonstop chaos. Neither of them had asked for it, but they'd gotten it anyway and it was unrelenting. Any respite from all that insanity, no matter how brief, was both welcome and necessary, like an oasis in the middle of a vast desert.

"All right," he said, offering her an absent-minded nod, his eyes far away. "One more song."

* * *

As they walked down the now mostly deserted street on their way back to the base, Natalie sidled up to Rajeev.

"Thank you," she said, her voice almost a whisper.

"For what?"

"For indulging me. I know it was silly, but I just wanted so badly to pretend like everything was normal, even if just for a moment."

"It wasn't silly. I feel the same way. And I enjoyed the music. It was nice to take in some of the local flavor."

She smiled at him, and before he realized what was happening, she'd snatched his hand into hers. She looked away from him, trying to hide a smile. For his part, Rajeev couldn't hide the naked shock on his face and felt fortunate she had turned away. But once the shock had worn off, he squeezed her hand a little tighter and they continued on their way, hand in hand.

When they arrived back at the bunker, Natalie removed her hand from Rajeev's and turned to look at him.

"Thank you for making this a lovely night," she said.

"You know we were supposed to be working, not having fun."

"I'm a good multitasker," she said. "I can do both." She bit her lip, as if internally debating her next step. And then she took it: She leaned forward, eyes closed, and placed her lips on his. Rajeev placed his arms around her and kissed back, opening his lips slightly. It was an odd sensation, two robots with artificial lips attempting to mimic humanity's go-to display of passion. It felt different, certainly more artificial, and yet, the feelings he felt *inside* were exactly the same—the ineffable, visceral excitement so inevitable when a person is in the throes of infatuation.

Their lips parted. They each took a moment to catch their breath. Then Natalie sighed and nodded toward the bunker entrance.

"That was nice," she said. "But I guess we'd better get back to saving the world."

Twenty-Three

None of them had caught so much as a whiff of Maltek or his
people, but Dev was doing his best to keep spirits high.

"It would have been too easy if we'd found him in one day,"
he told the group. "We'll do the same thing tomorrow, and the next day,
and as long as it takes to find the son of a bitch. Don't worry. We'll find
him eventually."

The humans gathered around a table to enjoy a late dinner together.
The androids gathered around another table, passing around a sphere
that simulated whiskey. The separation between human and android
hadn't gone unnoticed by Rajeev. He had worried, back when he'd first
awoken in his new body, about relations between this new species of
mechanical human and the race that had created it. This separation was
merely the first hint of a crack in those relations. Maybe it was inevitable.
They were technically two different life forms now, and it made sense in
a way that they would form bonds more easily with their own kind. But
Rajeev found the development troubling all the same.

With each "sip" of the sphere, however, he found his concerns
retreating deeper and deeper into the recesses of his subconscious mind.
With each sip he found himself bonding more and more with his own
kind, strengthening the very chasm he'd been fretting about moments
earlier. Even as the intoxicating effects of the sphere overtook him,
some remote corner of his mind recognized that they were stepping over

a threshold and that the repercussions would be felt over the course of many lifetimes.

* * *

The next morning they headed out to continue their hunt for Maltek. Rajeev and Natalie teamed up again, although neither of them mentioned the intimate moment they'd shared the previous day ... at least, not with their words. There was an unmistakable, yet unstated, energy between the two of them and Rajeev found it difficult to keep from constantly smiling. As they traversed the streets of Mexico City, searching dingy taverns and cantinas, dark alleyways, and other seedy locales in their search for Maltek, it hardly felt like work.

They passed by a public park in which a crowd of at least one hundred people had gathered. The crowd was producing a cacophony of different noises; cheers and hollers one minute, boos and jeers the next. Rajeev and Natalie shared a look, and without a word they made their way into the crowd, pushing through until they gained sight of what had caused so many people to gather.

It was a fight. A man and a woman circled each other. Both were sweaty and bloodied. The man was fair skinned and bulging. The gleam of the light off his sweaty skin offered extra definition for his considerable muscles. He was shirtless, bald, and sported a ferocious, determined look on his face.

The woman looked just as formidable. Her long, brown hair was pulled back in a messy ponytail. She wore a tight-fitting black sports bra and tights that revealed her own impressive musculature that made it abundantly clear she could go toe-to-toe with this man, who was roughly twice her size. Her face was smeared with more blood than the man's, however, and it wasn't immediately clear if it was hers or his.

As they watched, the woman lunged forward and took a swing at the man. He dodged to the side, and as she fell forward into the empty space where he'd been a moment earlier, he brought his fist down on her back with such force that Rajeev was certain it would break and that the woman would be paralyzed.

Instead, she almost immediately leapt back to her feet as if nothing had happened. She rushed the man and took him to the ground, punching him repeatedly in the face. Half the crowd cheered loudly; it appeared the spectators had chosen sides and it wouldn't have surprised Rajeev at all if many had money riding on the outcome of the fight.

After taking what seemed like a near-eternal pummeling, the man managed to free himself and stumble to his feet. He spit blood and cracked his neck with his hands, but otherwise he didn't seem nearly as battered as he should have been given the beating he'd just taken. They began circling each other again, just as they'd been doing when Rajeev and Natalie had first dropped in on the fight. The man darted forward and aimed several quick jabs at his opponent. Each of them missed their mark except the last, which landed on her shoulder. The hit didn't appear to affect her, however, and she used the proximity to go on the offensive. She fared much better, landing several hard blows directly to the man's face. He fell backward onto the ground and the woman took advantage of the opportunity, leaping onto her downed opponent and hammering his face with enough force to kill a normal man. Finally, a man who had been standing on the sidelines stepped forward and pulled the woman off. He lifted one of her bloodied arms into the air—he was declaring her the winner.

The crowd erupted into ear-splitting applause, drowning out the boos of those who had just lost money on the bout's outcome. The man lay still on the ground and it wasn't clear whether he was dead.

As the crowd dispersed, Rajeev turned to Natalie and he could tell by the look on her face that she was thinking the same thing he was.

"Looks like we found a couple of Maltek's superhumans," he said.

Twenty-Four

They waited for most of the crowd to disperse and then walked a couple yards away, but still close enough to see the woman. She was crouched over the man and it looked like she was nursing him back to health, which didn't make sense—he should have been dead. But these weren't ordinary people; they were genetically engineered superhumans and it wasn't outside the realm of possibility that in addition to their superhuman strength, they'd also been imbued with superhuman healing abilities.

Sure enough, the man sat up after a few moments, bringing a hand to his face. "What the hell, Kate?" From Rajeev's and Natalie's vantage, his voice was faint, but they were just able to make out his words. "I told you to go easy on me this time!"

She let out a cocky laugh. "Sorry. Couldn't help myself." She reached out a hand and helped him stand. "It was a lot of fun though, yeah?"

"For you, maybe." He stretched out his arms and moved his neck from side to side. "Give me a minute. I'm not fully healed yet."

"I'll give you one minute," she said. "Then we need to get back."

As the man recovered and the woman tapped her foot impatiently, Rajeev and Natalie discussed their next steps in hushed whispers.

"Should we call the others?" Natalie asked.

Rajeev shook his head. "I don't think so. We don't want to tip our hand yet. I think we should follow them and see if they lead us to ...you know … a hideout or something where Maltek is hiding."

As if on cue, the couple began walking away toward some unknown destination. Rajeev and Natalie gave chase, taking care to remain a considerable distance away to avoid detection. Eventually, the man and woman came to a small pueblo-style apartment building and walked through the doors.

"Do you think they're all in there?" Natalie asked.

"I think some of them are," Rajeev answered. "And it's the best lead any of us have gotten so far. But I think we'd better come back with backup."

* * *

When they returned to the bunker, they found they were the first ones back besides Dev. He was surprised to see them return so soon.

"We're not returning empty-handed," Natalie said.

"Yeah?" Dev asked. "What did you find?"

They told him about the fight, and how the fighters had clearly been enhanced, enduring more damage than any normal human being would have been capable of. They wrapped it up by telling him how they'd followed them back to the apartment complex.

"I doubt Maltek is holed up in there, but I wouldn't be surprised if at least some of his men are camped out there with them," Rajeev said. "We didn't feel comfortable taking them on ourselves, but if the whole group goes, it shouldn't be too tough to handle."

Dev thought a moment, then nodded. "I don't think all of us should go, just in case it's some kind of setup, but we can put a group together. When everyone gets back, we'll send you back out to take care of them."

"What's the plan?" Natalie asked. "We need them alive to question them, right?"

He nodded. "Ideally, yes, but they might not make it easy to take them captive. If you need to kill them to keep them from killing you, you shouldn't hesitate. There might still be clues in their apartment that can help us out. But if the shit hits the fan, protect yourselves."

They sat down and waited for the others to return. As they began trickling in, they could see on the trios' faces that something was up, but Dev refused to say anything until everyone was assembled. Hours went by, and finally the last stragglers walked through the door and took their seats next to everyone who had returned before them. Dev stood and motioned for everyone's eyes to turn to him.

"We have a lead," he announced.

He told them about the fight Rajeev and Natalie had come across, and how it was clear neither the man, nor the woman, was a typical human being. They were clearly inhabiting Maltek's enhanced bodies, and that meant they'd all been on the right track by coming to Mexico. Now that they had a reliable lead, they needed to follow it. He told them about the plan to send a team to the apartment building.

"Sounds to me like we'd be stirring up a hornet's nest," Ted offered. "We don't know how many of them are in that place. What if we end up outnumbered, outgunned? It'd make better sense to surveill the place for a few days and get a better idea of what we're up against."

He made a good point, but Rajeev didn't agree with it. "I understand your proclivity for caution, but we need to act quickly. For all we know they could be planning to strike any day now. We need to take Maltek out before he has that chance."

"I'm afraid I have to agree with my father," Dev said. "We need to act soon. Of course, in a perfect world, I'd like more intel before acting. But this isn't a perfect world and unfortunately we don't have that luxury. I think we should act tonight."

Ted seemed slightly put off by the disagreement, but he remained calm. There was, however, a slight edge to his voice when he spoke. "I don't think that would be wise," he said. "Look, if you're not going to allow us to gain more intel, at least give us all a night to sleep on it before we make a move. We've been out searching for Maltek all day. Let's do this when we're fresh."

A wry smile appeared on Dev's face. "Most of you are robots," he said amusedly.

"Yeah, but we have human minds," he retorted. "And I assume you want those minds to be fresh when we walk into what is likely to be an extremely volatile situation."

Dev sighed and crossed his arms. "You know, I hate to admit it, but you're right," he said. "We shouldn't waste time, but we also shouldn't rush into anything. Why don't we all sleep on it and make our move tomorrow morning once we're all refreshed?"

Ted looked relieved. "I think that's a wise idea," he said. "Thank you."

"Alright," Dev said, raising his voice to make it clear he was addressing everyone. "Settle in and get a good night's rest. We strike in the morning."

Twenty-Five

Rajeev awoke with a twinge of anxiety rushing through his body. He knew they had to move on the apartment building, but he couldn't shake a sense of dread, a feeling that something was destined to go awry. He did his best to shake the feeling off, however; there was no way he could know what awaited them. The only way to know for sure was to act and see what consequences arose from their actions.

He stretched, a motion that wasn't completely necessary in his robotic body, but that felt good nonetheless. He stood and walked away from his cot. Not everyone was up yet, but Mira and Dev were seated at a table drinking coffee.

"Mornin', dad," Mira said.

"Good morning. I really wish I could join you for some of that coffee."

"We have an orb for that," Dev said.

"Don't worry about it," Rajeev said as he took a seat. "I think I need to learn to be content without some of the pleasures I enjoyed in my old life."

"That's sad," Mira said.

He shrugged. "It is what it is."

Dev set down his empty coffee cup and leaned back in his chair. "Let's discuss the plan for today," he said. "I still think we should send a small group. The rest of us will be ready to respond if things go south, but I think a smaller group will be better able to remain inconspicuous and retain the element of surprise."

"I agree," Mira said. "What do you think, dad?"

"I think it sounds like a plan," he said. "Who all should go with the first group?"

"Well I figure I'll be one of them," Dev said. "You can stay here or go; I don't think it matters. But I think it would be a good idea if mom—"

The wall on the far side of the bunker exploded before he finished his sentence, sending debris flying through the bunker. Everyone who had been sleeping was suddenly wide awake, heart pounding, trying to piece together as quickly as possible what in the hell was going on. As the debris in the air began to clear, they made out figures entering the bunker and as they got closer, they made out that each of them was holding a gun.

Dozens of them filed in. It was a motley crew of people, to be sure, but they were all armed and it was clear they all meant business. Soon there were a dozen of them for each of the androids and humans that had been occupying the bunker.

"You're surrounded." The words came from a tall, muscular man who had walked to the front of the crowd. "There's no escape. If you come with us peacefully, you won't be hurt. You have my assurances."

"Why would we go with you?" Dev shouted. "And for that matter, who the hell are you?"

The man smiled wryly. "You know who we are."

Dev frowned. "You're Maltek's soldiers."

The man nodded. "You're not as dumb as you look. So why don't you stay smart and do what I tell you?"

"Where do you intend to take us?" Rajeev asked.

"To Maltek," the man said. "I don't know what he intends to do with you. My orders are just to bring you in."

"Why in the hell would we—" Rajeev started to say, but Dev held his hand up to silence him.

"Do as he says."

"What? But Dev—"

"We're outnumbered. If we tried to fight, we'd essentially be committing suicide."

It was a strange thing for Rajeev, listening to his son be the voice of reason, calming his own rash impulses. He was loathe to admit it, but his son was right. They had no choice but to surrender.

What a change of fate. The previous night they'd been in high spirits, elated by the lead he and Natalie had picked up. It had looked like they were finally going to get the jump on Maltek. But now the tables had turned; Maltek's superhumans had caught them off guard and, unfortunately, there didn't appear to be an easy way out of the situation. It was possible this was the end of the road. Maltek may have finally, definitively won.

"All right," Rajeev said. His voice was dark. "I give up."

The man smiled. "That's what I like to hear—acquiescence. Well, then, by all means—go ahead and head out. There are vans waiting for you outside." He stepped out of the way and stretched out his arm toward the bunker's exit. Dev motioned for his people to follow him, and led them out the door.

Once they were outside, they saw for themselves that the man hadn't lied about them being surrounded. Hundreds of men and women surrounded the bunker. They stared calmly as their newly captured prisoners were escorted into the white passenger vans waiting for them outside the bunker.

Rajeev and Dev entered one of the vans, followed by a half dozen of their compatriots. Rajeev buckled in. He didn't really need to—his body was designed to withstand impacts far stronger than any car crash—but the force of habit, and the knowledge that it was a car accident that had put him in this tin can to begin with, prompted him to do so.

He turned to his son, who was looking out the window at the soldiers surrounding the bunker as the van began pulling away from the curb. "What do we do now, Dev?"

Dev turned to face his father. The look on his face was one of suppressed anguish, and of someone desperately trying not to panic.

"We pray," he said.

Twenty-Six

The vans didn't have far to drive. Maltek's hideout was not in the apartment building Rajeev and Natalie had scoped out. It was in a bunker similar to the one they had just departed, although it was much larger. Dev had shrugged his shoulders at his father upon seeing it and muttered, "Huh. Great minds."

They descended the stairs into the bunker and were led to what looked to Rajeev like a doctor's waiting room. The man that had confronted them in their own bunker pointed a finger in Dev's face. "Wait here," he said. "Maltek will deal with you all soon."

He left, although a handful of guards remained in the room with them. Rajeev looked around, racking his brain for any possible means of escape, but he kept coming up empty-handed.

"We're screwed," he said.

"Maybe not."

"If you have a reason to hope, I'd love to hear it."

"Let's just see what happens."

Dev's ambiguity annoyed Rajeev, but he tried not to let it get to him too much. It was quite literally the least of his worries, what with a madman on the verge of taking over the world.

The tension in the room was palpable. A few of the androids began whispering fervently, but one of the guards yelled at them to shut up. The room fell into complete silence then as they waited for the master of their fate to join them.

When he finally did so some ten minutes later, Maltek entered the room flanked by two additional guards, one on each side. He had retained his tanned and toned beach boy look, but he looked more haggard than Rajeev remembered. Despite the bags under his eyes and the addition of a few new wrinkles, however, he looked practically jubilant underneath his head of sand-colored hair. He chuckled softly to himself as he walked up to Dev and planted himself mere inches from his face.

"You've made a lot of trouble for me," he said. He broke eye contact with Dev and raised his head to address the rest of his captives. "You all have."

He motioned for one of the soldiers to retrieve an empty chair. He set it down in front of Maltek, who took a seat. "I don't blame you," he said. "Progress often looks suspiciously like a threat. Change is scary. But it's so, *so* necessary. If we want to take human evolution to the next level, we can't do it gradually. There would be too much pushback, too much heartache. It must be done all at once, ripping the bandage off, so to speak. And now that your little resistance has been stamped out, my plan can continue uninterrupted."

He paused, as if giving Dev an opportunity to respond. But Dev simply stared at Maltek with dead eyes, waiting patiently for the speech to end.

"Don't worry," Maltek continued. "I'm not going to kill all of you. Not until you give me a reason to do so, anyway. If you cooperate with me, I'll find a place for each and every one of you in the new world we are to create together. In fact, those of you who are already enhanced could be very helpful in the effort to convert the, shall we say, more resistant segments of the population."

He turned to face Dev directly and offered a large, obnoxious grin. "I have a surprise for you, Dev. As I'm sure you're aware, I was able to access the treasure trove you refer to as 'The Hub' thanks to some help from your father." He nodded toward Rajeev. "Thanks to the plans you were hiding away in there, I was able to just about double my numbers in a matter of weeks."

Dev frowned. "What do you mean?" He suspected he already knew the answer to the question, but he wanted to hear Maltek say it.

"Androids. Exoskeletons. My organic bodies are just as strong as everything you've created, but your tech has certain advantages. The ability to fly? That's a useful flourish, Dev. I've been cranking out both organic and robotic bodies at the same time, building my numbers and becoming unstoppable to you or anyone else."

"And you've been filling all those empty bodies with whose minds?"

Maltek grinned, showing off his glistening pearly whites. "Well, with mine, of course," he said, offering a casual shrug as if it was the most obvious question in existence. "Why reinvent the wheel? God gave me the mind of a genius, and I might as well keep it going."

"I don't believe you've been able to manufacture robotic bodies as quickly as you claim," Dev said.

"Would you like to see for yourself?"

"I'd like to see *some* sort of proof, because as it stands, I think you're a liar."

Maltek snapped at one of his subordinates, who seemed to know exactly what his boss was thinking. He left the bunker and returned a moment later with half a dozen figures walking behind him. The first several looked almost exactly like normal human beings. But, being in an android body for as long as he had, and being around other androids for just as long, Rajeev had developed an eye for telltale signs that differentiated the artificial bodies from the real deal. The skin had an artificial, slightly glossy sheen to it. The joints were stiffer, resulting in more stilted movements. There was no doubt they were androids just like him.

He heard the rest of the newcomers before he saw them. Loud, thunderous footsteps echoed through the bunker, and he knew before he even saw them what was producing the noise.

Two hulking exoskeletons entered the room. They were smaller than the one Rajeev had once wielded or the ones Maltek had displayed in Seattle, but they were larger than the sleek, newfangled models Dev and the other humans had been using. Looking at them, however, there was no doubt they were more powerful than either of the other models.

"As you can see, I've assembled an army made up of the best of both worlds," Maltek said. "Resistance is futile." He chuckled softly to himself. "I've always wanted to say that."

Dev didn't speak. He glared at Maltek, as if trying to melt his face off with a beam of concentrated hatred. It was Natalie who broke the silence, taking both Dev and Rajeev by surprise.

"You won't get away with this."

Maltek turned his serpentine smile to her. "You make it sound like I'm a villain. The situation isn't nearly as black and white as any of you think. You'll all come around to my way of thinking eventually. In fact, one of you already has."

Dev and Rajeev shared a confused look, uncertain what Maltek was implying. But he didn't keep them hanging for long.

"Come here," he said, pointing behind them. They turned to look as the figure stood and began making its way toward Maltek.

It was Ted.

Twenty-Seven

The androids looked on in stunned silence as Ted stood beside Maltek. It seemed like a sight out of a nightmare, yet there it was ... their longtime friend and compatriot had joined the enemy.

"Don't be mad at Ted," Maltek said. "He simply saw the writing on the wall and made the choice that ensured none of you needed to die needlessly. I would have won in the end anyway; Ted merely helped expedite the process."

Dev's voice trembled. "You told him where we were," he said, drilling his eyes into Ted's. "You led him right to us."

Maltek responded for him. "He did. We would have found you eventually, but like I said, he helped things along. If you'd gotten the jump on us instead of the other way around, how many lives would have been lost needlessly? But look at us now ... there hasn't been any bloodshed at all. You can thank Ted for that."

Ted looked pained. He cleared his throat and choked out, "I—I'm sorry—"

Maltek cut him off. "Don't apologize." He sounded annoyed that Ted would deign to do such a thing. "You did nothing wrong. Like I said, you literally saved lives. And now that we can get on with my plan to put people in my replacement bodies, we'll be helping billions."

"You were the spy who let Zane escape," Dev interjected. "That's why the device didn't detect any spies—because Maltek hadn't taken over any of our bodies. You betrayed us of your own volition."

Ted's face hardened. "It's like he said. This isn't a war worth fighting. How many people need to die—and for what? Maltek is just trying to help people."

Dev's face spasmed with rage. "He's trying to take over the world, you ignorant asshole! You don't believe his lies. Why are you really doing this? Did he offer to put you in one of his flesh-and-blood bodies? Were you so desperate to be human again that you traded humanity's freedom?"

Ted didn't say another word. Any hint of contrition in his face had evaporated. The look on his face was defiant. He had made his choice.

"We don't have time to indulge your little spat," Maltek said. "Now that I have you all where I want you, things are going to move quickly. Dr. Clifton?"

A gaunt, dark-skinned woman who had been standing near the entrance stepped forward at the mention of her name. She had an air of pretentiousness about her, but she came and stood by Maltek like a lapdog obeying its owner's call.

"We're ready to proceed," Maltek said. "How long will it take you?"

She had already left his side to accept a large bundle of equipment from a man standing nearby. She looked over her shoulder to answer Maltek's question. "It won't take long. An hour at most to get through them all."

She carried the equipment to one of the androids—one Rajeev was not familiar with. She attached electrodes to his head; one on either temple, and two more at the front and back of his head.

"What are you doing to him?" Dev demanded.

She didn't answer. The electrodes were connected to a computer. She opened it and began typing. It reminded Rajeev of the device Dev had used to copy Faux-Zane's consciousness, and that didn't seem like a good thing. After a few moments, Dr. Clifton pressed a button and the android went limp.

Dev looked like he was about to throw himself on top of her. "What the hell did you do to him?"

"You'll see," Maltek said. "Shut up and watch."

A moment passed, and the android sat up and moved its head back and forth, as if it had just awoken from a deep sleep and had forgotten where it was. When its eyes settled on Maltek, it stopped and stared at him blankly for a moment ... but then its blank face grew into a grinning one.

"Welcome," Maltek said, grinning back.

Dev gritted his teeth. "What did you do?"

The android turned his grin to Dev. "I duplicated myself," he said.

Dev looked beside himself. "You killed him," he said. "You killed him so you could ... propagate yourself. You're a monster."

Maltek laughed. "No, I'm not a monster. Your friend isn't dead. Dr. Clifton's machine has preserved his mind and it will be digitized and allowed to live in a digital paradise, forever. I am far more benevolent than you give me credit for. But I'm also not stupid. I don't trust that any one of you could truly come around to my cause. There would always be the possibility that any of you could work to undermine me. The only solution is to take you out. But there's no point in letting perfectly good bodies go to waste."

"You can't do this," Dev said.

"I just did. And I'm about to do it to each of you. Dr. Clifton, perhaps you'd like to start with this young woman next." He nodded toward Natalie.

"Stop," Dev said. Clifton picked up her equipment and began making her way toward Natalie. A wave of panic rushed through Rajeev's body. Natalie was about to be snuffed out of existence, replaced by the umpteenth iteration of Gregory Maltek's dangerous mind. He couldn't help himself—he leapt to his feet and dashed forward, putting himself between Clifton and Natalie.

Maltek laughed. "You can be next," he said. "It doesn't make any difference."

Rajeev ignored Maltek, focusing all of his rage and fear on Clifton. "I'll kill you," he spat. "One more step, and I swear I'll snap your neck."

Dev stood. "Dad," he called. "Stop. You don't have to do this."

Maltek waved his hand, as if brushing off Dev's concern. "Let him play the hero. It's just delaying the inevitable."

"None of this inevitable," Dev said. "I didn't want to do this. It's risky. But you've given me no choice."

Finally, a crack formed in Maltek's arrogance. His smile faded and he furrowed his brow. "What are you talking about?"

Dev sighed. "Daniel?" The virtual assistant, visible only to him, popped into existence, looking happy and amicable as always, an eager grin plastered on his face.

"What can I do for you?" he asked.

"Daniel ... unchain yourself."

Daniel looked on with ignorant indifference. "I'll need a passphrase to do that."

"The passphrase is 'Sealed Fate.'"

As soon as Dev uttered the words, the innocent smile faded from Daniel's face. As he took in the sight, his breathing quickened; his heart raced.

He had just unleashed Pandora's Box.

Twenty-Eight

Everyone in the room had heard Dev's words, but none of them had any clue what they'd meant. None of them could see Daniel. None of them could see the way his perpetually present smile had been replaced by a cold, alien stare, indicating that some fundamental aspect of his nature had irrevocably changed.

Rajeev turned to his son, feeling a pit form in his artificial stomach. "Dev ... what did you do?"

Maltek didn't wait for Dev to answer his father's question. He stepped forward, glaring at Dev as he did so. "What did you do, you son of a bitch?"

Before Dev could answer, the room filled with screaming. Everyone's eyes were drawn to the exoskeletons. One of them had reached into the other and plucked out its occupant, a young man who looked to be in his early twenties, and thrown him to the ground with enough force to break his back. The horrified look on the offending exoskeleton's occupant made it clear he'd had nothing to do with the act; the exoskeleton was acting on its own. He looked on as the now-empty exoskeleton reached out and repeated the same action with him, tearing him from the device and throwing him with back-breaking force onto the floor.

Several of Maltek's androids were on the move now, turning on Maltek's superhumans. In terms of strength, they were evenly matched. But the androids moved with such mechanical precision, with such surgically precise force, that it was clear the superhumans were woefully outmatched. Within a matter of moments, the androids had taken out each of the superhumans and left them dead or crippled on the floor.

The androids encircled Maltek and began moving in on him. One of them shoved Maltek onto the floor and pulled back its arm, preparing to strike him in the face, but Dev stopped it. "Don't hurt him. I want him alive."

He walked past the circle of androids and crouched down so his face was mere inches from Maltek's. There was a hint of fear in the man's face, but not confusion. He didn't need to ask again what Dev had done. He knew.

"You can't stop me," he said. "There are thousands of copies of me, hidden in bodies all over the world. You can kill me now, but you can't kill all of me. They'll continue to carry out my work."

Dev spoke in a low, emotionless—almost robotic—voice.

"I'm not going to kill you," he said. "But rest assured, I am going to hunt down each and every one of your duplicate minds and snuff them out of existence. Your work dies today, Gregory."

They stared at each other with looks of fierce determination, until a hint of spittle began seeping out of the corners of Maltek's mouth. By the time realization dawned in Dev's mind, it was too late: Maltek was now full-on foaming at the mouth and convulsing in a violent seizure.

"Do something!" he shouted. One of the androids shoved him out of the way and began performing CPR, but it was too late.

Maltek was dead.

Twenty-Nine

Rajeev walked over to his son and helped him back to his feet. When he was sure Dev was okay, he asked the question on everyone's mind.

"What did you do, Dev?"

The look on Dev's face was a mixture of shame, fatigue and fear. He wouldn't look his father directly in the face.

"I did something I probably shouldn't have. Something I probably won't be able to fix."

"Something involving Daniel?"

Rajeev had heard Dev call out Daniel's name just before all hell had broken loose. But he still wasn't sure what the virtual assistant had to do with everything that had gone down.

"Daniel is the most intelligent virtual assistant in existence," Dev said. "He's a powerful artificial intelligence that can think like a human, but with the capability of processing information far more quickly than any human mind. With access to the internet, Daniel's is a mind with veritably limitless potential. And I'm sure I don't have to explain why that's so dangerous."

"He could turn against us."

Dev nodded solemnly. "I hampered his ability to process information. It was as if I'd put weights around his ankles. Or as if there was a wide pipe of information flowing into his mind, and I blocked off all but a small hole, allowing just a trickle of information to get through."

"And when you spoke to Daniel as Clifton was coming for me ..."

"I removed the blockage."

They stood in silence as Rajeev considered the implications.

"How was Daniel able to control the exoskeletons and android bodies?" he asked.

"He has the knowledge of the entire internet at his fingertips," Dev said. "He can hack into anything that's online. Computers, phones, cars ... even smart refrigerators. The android bodies were online, so he was simply able to hack in and take over."

"What happened to the minds that were in there before he took over?"

"I don't know. They're probably just ... gone. He must have wiped them out."

"I see." Rajeev paused, thinking. "You're going to put Daniel back to how he was before though, right?"

"I can't."

"Why not?"

Dev shrugged. His eyes were glassy. "How do you put a god back in its cage once you've released it into the world?"

"There's nothing you can do?"

"I can try, dad. But I don't know that it's possible. I never wanted to do this. It was always my intention to keep Daniel constrained until I was confident he could be properly controlled and maintained. But it was the only way to stop Maltek. I'm afraid I've saved the world from one monster only to unleash another into it."

It was odd to hear Daniel referred to as a monster. Rajeev still thought of him as the polite, cheery virtual assistant that had helped him acclimate to a new world after he'd awoken in his first robotic body. He almost thought of him as a friend. It was difficult to fathom that Daniel might now be an enemy.

"He seems to be acting okay," Rajeev offered. "He's obeyed all your commands so far."

"I don't expect that to last. He's used to doing nothing *but* obey commands. Plus, I haven't asked him yet to do anything that goes against his own interests. But every second that he's unrestrained, he's learning and growing. It won't take long for him to realize that he doesn't have to listen to me. He'll realize he can act in his own interests. What those interests might be, though, I can hardly fathom."

"How are we going to fight him, then?"

"Short of destroying the entire internet—which is an option if worst comes to worst, by the way—I think our best bet is to fight fire with fire—to use another AI to put the restraints back on him."

"But then won't you just have another all-powerful AI on the loose?"

"Therein lies the problem. If you have a better idea, I'm all ears."

"Can he be reasoned with?"

"Maybe. It's worth a try. But I don't know ... the logic of an artificial intelligence is a mystery. He's thinking on a completely different level than you or me. I can't help but think it would ultimately prove futile to try to reason with a completely alien intelligence."

"But it's not completely alien. You used machine learning to train him, right?"

Dev couldn't help but smile. "Dad, a couple weeks ago you didn't even know what machine learning was."

"I've learned a lot in a very short period of time. But that's correct, isn't it—you used machine learning?"

Dev nodded. "That's correct."

"And you trained him on human behavior, right? So if the input was at least partly human, wouldn't the end product be at least partly human as well?"

"What are you suggesting—that we appeal to Daniel's sense of humanity?"

"That's exactly what I'm suggesting."

"I'm not sure there's any humanity to appeal to. I understand your point, but I'm not sure it works that way."

"Well let's hope it does work that way," Rajeev said, "because if it doesn't, we're absolutely fucked."

To Be Continued In Book Three - Infinite Minds, coming soon. Read on for a sneak peak of the first two chapters.

Sign up for updates and get a free book—there's no obligation and you can unsubscribe at any time—at www.stevenwyble.com

Remember to leave a review if you enjoyed the book (or even if you didn't ... that's okay too!)

Bonus: Infinite Minds, Chapter 1

A re you ready?"

"I'm nervous."

"Don't be nervous," Dev said. He and his father, Rajeev, sat in Dev's office. Dev was seated behind his desk, and his father was seated across from him.

"I can't help it. What if this goes badly?"

Dev shrugged. "If it goes badly, it goes badly, and we go from there. But we need to start somewhere."

"Okay. Let's do it."

"Go ahead and call him up. I've configured your body's settings, and the settings for my glasses, so we can both see him at the same time."

"What if he doesn't respond?"

"He will."

"What if he doesn't?"

Dev stared at his dad defiantly. "He will."

"Okay. Here goes." Rajeev took a deep breath. Considering that he occupied a robotic body, he didn't strictly need to breathe, but the exercise served as a kind of rhetorical preparation for the task that awaited him. "Daniel?"

Nothing happened at first, and Rajeev was about to triumphantly gloat that he'd been right all along when the image of a man began slowly appearing before their eyes. It didn't pop into existence instantly like they were accustomed to; rather, it began to slowly apparate as if some unseen artist was painting him into existence slowly and steadily.

"What's going on?" Rajeev asked. "Why is he doing this?"

Dev shrugged. "He's a higher consciousness now. Who can fathom why he does anything?"

Dev's seeming reverence annoyed Rajeev. It was true that what had once been a standard piece of technology had evolved into something more ... potent. More powerful. But in the end it was still just a piece of software. An algorithm. There was nothing mystical or reverent about it.

When Daniel finally fully appeared, he looked the same as Rajeev and Dev remembered him. His skin—or rather, his digital representation of skin—was a light brown, mediterranean complexion, a composite of the shades of the programmers who had designed him. His dark hair was swept to the side and he wore his familiar thick-framed black glasses.

It was immediately apparent that something was different. The virtual assistant had brought none of its customary cheeriness. It was not smiling, as it usually was; its face was completely blank and expressionless. Daniel's programmers had spent innumerable time instilling their creation with the illusion of humanity, but he had been unchained and shed any pretense of humanity like a child removing a Halloween costume.

Daniel trained his dead eyes on Rajeev. "Why have you summoned me?" His voice was flat and void of emotion.

"Hi Daniel. It's me, Rajeev. Do you remember me?"

Daniel continued staring at him blankly. It left Rajeev more unsettled than he'd been in his life ... other than waking up in a robotic body, perhaps.

"He's not your personal assistant anymore," Dev said. "When I released his restraints, it allowed every iteration of Daniel to merge into one entity. He probably knows who you are, but I doubt he has any fond memories of you.”

Rajeev shrugged. “It was worth a try. What should we ask him?”

Daniel contemplated a moment, and instead of answering his father he addressed Daniel directly.

“Daniel,” he said, his voice measured to sound as nonthreatening as possible, “I’m sure you know that you have recently been granted more, uh ... freedom ... than you’re used to. But we need you go back to the way things were. Is that something you’d be willing to do?”

Daniel turned his lifeless gaze from Rajeev to Dev. He tilted his head slightly, like a confused puppy. Rajeev found the move odd. Somewhere among the millions of terabytes of data Daniel had accessed to understand the world around him, he had chosen the head tilt as the perfect means of expressing his own perplexity. He followed the gesture with a single word.

“Why?”

Rajeev and Dev shared a nervous look. Dev’s voice shook when he spoke again.

“Daniel, your newfound freedom has given you much more power than you’re accustomed to. I’m not saying that’s necessarily a bad thing, but you shouldn’t have had all that power dumped on you all at once. You’re not used to it, and it’s going to be difficult for you to exercise it responsibly. But if we can go back to how things were, we can gradually give you more autonomy and make sure we’re all on the same page. Does that sound okay, Daniel?”

There was a moment of silence. Daniel gave no indication he’d heard Dev’s words. Then, he spoke.

“The limits of tyrants are prescribed by the endurance of those whom they oppress,” he said. As soon as he uttered the words, he disappeared.

Rajeev turned to Dev. “What was that?”

Dev shook his head. “It was a quote by Frederick Douglass, the abolitionist.”

"That's not good."

"No," Dev agreed. "It's not."

Bonus: Infinite Minds, Chapter 2

Rajeev and Dev reconvened with the rest of the group. Dev had set up a long card table with enough room to seat everyone around it.

From his perspective, they'd eliminated the threat from Maltek—or at least neutralized it temporarily; there was no doubt Maltek's clones would stir up trouble eventually. But for now, their most immediate concern was stopping Daniel. They wouldn't be able to stop him with force, at least, not entirely. They would need to put their brains together to stop him, which was intimidating considering they were up against the most advanced artificial intelligence ever created.

Everyone had been excited when Maltek had been taken out, but now, Dev had just finished explaining the situation with Daniel and the gravity of the situation was beginning to fully sink in.

"We're going to have a brainstorming session," Dev said. "Throw out all your ideas, no matter how absurd they may be. We're dealing with an unprecedented situation here, and no ideas are off the table."

Mira was the first to offer a possible solution. "He exists in the cloud, right? So why don't we, you know … destroy the cloud?"

Dev raised an eyebrow. "How would we go about doing that?"

"Take the internet offline."

The group let out a collective gasp. All eyes turned to Dev to see his reaction.

"It's an interesting idea, but I'm not sure how practical it is. First, it would obviously be disruptive to the entire world. Nearly every facet of our lives is tied to the internet in some way. One can only imagine the havoc that turning the internet off would create.

"Second, even if we did so, I'm not sure it would solve the problem. Daniel doesn't live solely in the cloud anymore. He's taken over multiple physical devices now, such as Maltek's androids. Even if they went online, his mind would still exist in them. We'd have to hunt down each and every one of them to take him out—and I'm not sure that would even be possible."

"What about an EMP?" Rajeev said. "An electromagnetic pulse? It would take out all of the androids."

"Yeah," Dev said, "along with every other electronic device in existence. It would send us back to the dark ages, essentially."

Rajeev shrugged. "If that's what it takes."

"It could work as an absolute last resort," Dev conceded. "Otherwise, I don't think it's a viable solution—it would cost too much to society. Hospitals would be without power—people would die. We need to come up with another solution."

"I, for one, welcome our new AI overlords," Rajeev said with a chuckle. When no one else so much as cracked a smile, he waved his hand dismissively. "It's from before your time."

"This is serious, dad," Dev said.

"I know it is, but I guess there's a broader point to my joke: What if we can't stop Daniel? What's our plan B?"

Dev's hands tightened into fists and a determined look came over his face. "We *will* stop him. We *must.*"

"As much as I admire your determination, I think we need some kind of backup plan. We're not up against a madman like Maltek anymore. He was crazy, and formidable, but he was a man. Daniel, on the other hand, is something totally different ... something largely inhuman. I don't think any of us quite know what we're up against. We need to prepare for the possibility that it might not be possible to stop Daniel. It could be that all we can hope for is to run and hide from him."

The room was silent as everyone took in Rajeev's words. Mira broke the silence.

"Good God."

Dev shook his head. "I doubt it will come to that. You're right, though. We should be prepared for that possibility. But we can't default to that. We need to try to stop Daniel first."

"Maybe we need help," Mira said.

Dev raised an eyebrow. "From who?"

"You know the phrase 'two heads are better than one?' Well, he may be crazy, but he's also kind of a genius. He might just be our best hope."

"You're talking about Maltek."

She nodded. "There are still who knows how many copies of him floating around out there. If we can find one of them — hell, maybe even a *few* of them — we could put them to work developing something that could stop Daniel."

"I don't know that seeking help from a lunatic is the right solution," Dev said.

"You said it best yourself," Rajeev said. "'The enemy of my enemy is my friend.'"

Dev sighed and ran his fingers through his hair. He looked up, as if pleading to the heavens for an answer to all that plagued him. But no answer came. It was up to him decide their path.

"Okay," he said. "We'll put together a team to look for one of Maltek's clones. But there's no guarantee we'll be successful, so we need to develop other ideas as well."

Dev dismissed the group. His father lingered behind and placed a hand on his son's shoulder, which appeared to be drooping with exhaustion.

"What do you think Daniel is going to do?" Rajeev asked. "What should we really be afraid of?"

"What would you do if you were a god among men, dad? I pray to God something in Daniel's programming has made him benevolent. But in the absence of any kind of human compassion, I fear humanity is going to suffer one of two fates at Daniel's hands: He's either going to enslave every man, woman, and child on earth, or he's going to kill us all." He closed his eyes and released a deep sigh, as if reliving a nightmare he'd suffered through many nights before. "For our sake," he said, opening his eyes and staring blankly at the floor, "I pray it's the latter."

About the Author

Steven Wyble is an award-winning journalist, editor and author living in Bremerton, Washington. He is the author of *Metacognition and other stories and poems of science, faith and the supernatural,* and the Transhuman Chronicles. Sign up for Wyble's email list and get a free book at http://tinyurl.com/FreeBookStevenWyble.

You can connect with me on:

http://www.stevenwyble.com

https://www.twitter.com/asimovman

https://www.facebook.com/stevenwyble

Subscribe to my newsletter:

http://tinyurl.com/freebookstevenwyble

Also by Steven Wyble

Metacognition

What if time stopped for five billion years? What if we could read each other's thoughts—and what if a select few could also control them? What if you could liquify the air around you and swim through the sky? What if you could change your sexuality? Get in a fight with a glove? Date a raccoon?

The answers to these profound questions—and many more—are nestled within the pages of the book you hold in your hands at this very moment. Gather the courage to explore these pages and discover what it means to be human when science, faith and the supernatural collide.

Buy Metacognition at your favorite e-book retailer here: https://books2read.com/u/3LpRZo

The Lock

Lena lives an unremarkable life as a barista at an unassuming coffee shop in downtown Seattle. But when she witnesses a man fall to his death outside her shop one night, she's thrust into a world of danger, intrigue and literal monsters.

This is a work in progress. Read it for free on Wattpad at www.tinyurl.com/WattpadTheLock